TIMESNATCHED

POLE STAR

B.D. BOYLE

U.S. $10.50

© 2013 B.D. Boyle
© 2020 Revised Edition B.D. Boyle

All rights reserved.

No part of this book may be reproduced in any form whatsoever whether by graphic, visual or electronic, film, microfilm, tape recording or any other means without prior

written permission of the publisher, except in the case of brief passages embodied in critical reviews and articles.

This book is a work of fiction. Any references to historical events, real people or races are used fictitiously. Other names, characters, places, and events are products
of the author's imagination, and any resemblance to actual events or places or persons, living or dead, is purely coincidental.

ISBN-13: 978-1493531554

Copyright Cover Design 2013 Rebecca Moorhouse
Printed in the United States of America

*To Derek,
for believing in my stories*

Prologue

Questions bombarded Nicolas Wycliffe as he stared at the time machine prototype in the palm of his hand. *How does Grandpa think he can help Molly? He's attempting the impossible!*

Nicolas lifted his eyes to the golden red glare of the London night sky. In the minutes he had been standing there, the shrill scream of bombs hurling toward the earth had overpowered the drone of the Nazi bombers. The ground under his feet shuddered and he quickly slipped the prototype, no bigger than a pocket watch, into the safety of his coat pocket. He saw a sign on the street corner and sprinted for the stairway of the London Underground. His long legs took him to the subterranean tube that wound under London proper. Vast numbers of people crouched in the semi-darkness, seeking shelter from the Blitz that was showering London with fire and exploding bombs. The firestorm above was sucking the city of its precious oxygen; but down there, in the depths of the Underground, Nicolas Wycliffe found relative safety—at least for now.

After raking his fingers through his unruly cowlick, Nicolas attempted to wipe from his thick glasses the black soot from the war zone above. He glanced around at the poor souls who cowered nearby and then sank to the floor, his back to the stone wall. This was the night he had read about in history books; the night his grandfather had told him about so often that Nicolas could have recited the tale by heart. "It was a scene from the bowels of hell, to be sure." His grandfather described the fateful night of December 29, 1940. "I was with my cousin and childhood friend, Molly McGruder. We were running through the streets of London, half expecting a bomb to land on us at any moment." The old man often paused and reflected at that point in the story. His eyes looked up as if watching the scene on a giant screen. "Molly stumbled and fell; I reached out to help her when the brick wall of a building fell on her, throwing me ten yards away into a pile of rubble. I ran to her, but I knew it was too late. My dear friend and cousin was gone from my life."

Nicolas sighed. Here he was in London on that horrific night in 1940, trying to find his grandfather who had taken one of two prototypes of the time machine he had invented just two months before. Nicolas himself had not even had a chance to test the little machine properly before he discovered that one was missing. From journal entries he knew exactly where his grandfather was headed. And, thanks to the history books, he knew *when*. A quick Internet search revealed the GPS coordinates of the warehouse that had fallen and he drove to the location for the time jump.

There was a momentary hush in the Underground. All eyes turned to the ceiling. Nothing. Nicolas jumped up to take advantage of the lull. When he emerged on the surface once again, he glanced at the map he had saved on his cellphone and took off running. In minutes, he was on Shoe Lane. Firemen were training a fire hose on a burning book factory amidst the penetrating heat. People were shouting and the ever-present pungent odor of smoke billowed high into the sky. Nicolas searched the alleyways and down every sidewalk. Coughing, he ran until his lungs were bursting. He leaned over, hands on his knees, to take a rest and then he saw them—two teenagers running hand-in-hand. One was unmistakably the teen version of Nicolas' grandfather, for he had seen his boyhood pictures many times. The other was a girl in school uniform with curly, red hair. Her pretty freckled face was etched with fear. She must be Molly McGruder, Grandpa's cousin, thought Nicolas. He stood in the smoky shadows observing the pair when from around the corner a tall, lanky old man rapidly approached the couple—in his hand was the time machine prototype.

"Grandpa, no!" shouted Nicolas.

The grandfather ignored the warning and thrust the prototype into the boy's hand. Suddenly, a large portion of the tall, brick building broke free from the roof structure. Nicolas watched in horror as the massive wall descended toward the helpless trio below. At that instant, a firebomb lit up the street like a giant flare and the three victims disappeared just as the bricks landed in a massive pile on the street. Nicolas pursed his lips, reached into his pocket for his time machine and whispered, "Grandpa, what in the world have you done?"

One

Jack Flint really didn't need anybody's help. He was smart and could figure things out on his own. Like the time his dad had run errands and left him at the ranch. He wasn't surprised that their heifer who was about to calve chose that afternoon to do it. She was bellowing and snorting and kicking up dust. The challenge would have daunted a much older man, let alone a 17-year-old boy.

"How hard can this be?" mumbled Jack. He dug back in his memory to last year's calving season when he worked at his father's side. He swore a few times, but in the end, the calf made it out alive and the cow seemed grateful. When his dad returned, he took his hat off, scratched his head and said, "Good thing you were with me last year. Here, there's chickens to feed."

Jack Flint was a respectful boy. He carried the flag with dignity in the Rattlesnake Wash Fourth of July parade, let his granny ramble on about her hip surgery, and never swore around the little kids. His chores on the ranch were always done on time and he usually complimented his mother on her good, home-cooked meals. His ten brothers and sisters looked up to Jack as the older brother who could fix anything from a broken sling shot to a messed-up computer program. And, he liked to tease.

But, Jack had one challenge. Some people would call it a virtue, but the quality plagued Jack almost every day of his life. He had a keen sense of right and wrong that would make a district judge look like a crook. The problem came at school with his friends who got tired of him being so squeaky clean.

Last fall was a good example. Jack stood alone, for at least a few minutes, the day there was an after-school fight. The warring parties had agreed to meet at the vacant lot over by the drive-in theater to settle their differences. It was after school and they had had all day to think about it. Tempers were flaring. Just when the crowd was expecting the biggest guy to throw the first punch, he pulled a gun from under his vest. The crowd froze.

Jack knew in a flash what he was going to do. He reached into his pick-up truck, retrieved his .22 rifle and leveled it at the troublemaker. "This is supposed to be a fair fight, Johnson, and it's going to *be* a fair fight. Now, drop it!"

Johnson defiantly stood his ground.

The crowd tensed. The minutes passed. Jack looked to his friends for aid, but they were mostly staring at the ground, kicking at the dirt. The Johnson kid got brave and when he cocked his pistol, the click echoed in the silence. Jack continued aiming with his steel-gray eyes and stood firm. And then, there wasn't just one 17-year-old boy making a determined point—there were now four, then six, then eight others standing beside him, each with a rifle aimed at Johnson. He looked up, turned a rather deep shade of cherry red and skulked off to his car.

"Thanks, you guys," said Jack humbly, as he patted several on the back. "I've only shot ground squirrels with that thing. Glad that hasn't changed."

The next day at school, everyone was abuzz over the rumble of the previous afternoon. The jocks in the high school quietly congratulated Jack for his quick thinking. And, not a few girls looked in his direction.

Jack spent most of noon hour describing the events of the almost fight. He gave most of the credit to his stalwart supporters, the true friends who showed up with rifles they used exclusively for squirrel hunting after school. Jack drew devoted friends like a magnet, the kind of friends that admired the causes he always seemed drawn to.

And so, when Sheriff Cooke needed an extra hand one Friday night, he gave Jack a call and asked him to ride along. Jack hadn't made a secret of his admiration of law enforcement work and relished the chance to spend the evening with the sheriff. Sheriff Cooke liked Jack and having the boy along would serve to keep him awake, at least until midnight when Jack's folks wanted him home.

Nothing much happened in the sleepy little valley that lay at the foot of the Teton mountain range. Winters were harsh and most people were up at the ski lodge or watching TV around the wood stove. But, this was summertime and it was different. The area attracted tourists and nature bums. Neither were much of a threat to valley security, but there had been some vandalism and the sheriff wanted to check out a few vacant, summer homes. It was about ten p.m. and they were headed south on Highway 33 when the dispatcher came over the radio.

"311 Teton."

"Go ahead," replied the sheriff.

"Got a 911 call on a moose versus car on Highway 31, mile marker 17. The moose is still in the road but no injuries to the driver."

"10-4. I'm southbound on 33. ETA ten minutes."

"2200," signed off the dispatcher.

The sheriff switched on his emergency lights but no siren. Jack perked up out of his almost catnap and hoped the sheriff hadn't noticed. Finally, something was happening. He felt himself pushed back in the seat as the sheriff accelerated the police SUV. In less than ten minutes, they were coming up to the reported accident.

Several cars had backed up, but the sheriff swerved around them on the gravel shoulder and soon they were staring at the car that had hit the moose. The animal was not dead and was sitting up in the middle of the highway. It was struggling to get to its feet, but repeatedly fell back down. At least one leg was broken.

"Jack, you feel like putting this one down?" Sheriff Cooke motioned toward the SUV and didn't wait for Jack to answer. "Get the 30.06 from the back."

Jack nodded and ran to the back of the police vehicle. He was no stranger to the procedure for putting down an injured animal. The quicker he put the moose out of its misery, the better. At least, that's what he had always been taught.

After quickly loading the rifle, Jack glanced once at Sheriff Cooke for the go-ahead and one single shot rang out over the valley. Jack took no pleasure in killing the injured moose but there were just some things that had to be done. He judged by the way a man about ten feet away was wringing his hands that he was the driver of the car. Jack withheld his judgment—there was nothing so hard to spot on a dark, moonless night than a black moose crossing the highway, even with your bright lights on.

Well, the task was done and that was that, thought Jack. He shouldered the rifle for the return to the police vehicle, its lights still flashing in the dark. He had just placed the weapon in its bracket when he felt a hand on his shoulder. He turned to see a man in a long, blue coat.

"Might I have a moment of your time?"

"Sure," replied Jack.

There was a gold pocket watch with an image of the world inscribed on it. It was in the palm of the man's hand and that's all that Jack Flint remembered—that and the flashing blue and red lights of the Teton County Sheriff's SUV.

Two

The day Annabelle Dibble was snatched into time dawned like any other summer day in Wigan, England. Sunlight had kissed her cheek early that morning and she looked at the clock. Seven a.m. and Aunt Tess had probably already left for work. In an hour, she was to meet Gemma at Wigan's Pier.

Annie slipped into the simple cotton skirt and blouse from the day before. She stood before the old dresser mirror as she fashioned her dark blonde hair back from her face and into a long braid which fell to the middle of her back. As she made her bed, thoughts of Wigan's Pier flooded her mind—the beautiful lawns, the smells of the quaint shops and the serene breeze off the canal. Gemma would be on Potter's Bridge. They would walk along the pier, linked arm-in-arm, and giggle at silly school-girl things and then plop down on the grass to share their latest reading adventures.

Annie headed for the kitchen and shoved a bagel into the toaster. Next to the telephone, she saw a letter with familiar handwriting. It was from her father, and she slipped it into her large, floppy handbag along with several library books.

"You're not goin' again! Please, Miss, stay 'round today," said a ruddy-cheeked little girl with blonde pigtails. The child was looking up from beneath the table.

"Can't stay, little Gertie—got to meet up with Gemma soon, besides you have plenty of playmates on this block. Now, eat the breakfast your mum's fixed for you."

Frowning, the girl climbed up on the nearest chair in time to watch Annie stuff her bag with more bagels, fruit from the basket, and two water bottles. There was a bang from the kitchen door as Annie waved goodbye and left.

The brilliant sunshine warmed Annie's back as she made her way down the sidewalk past the two-story row houses on Abbey Drive. She greeted the shopkeeper out sweeping his sidewalk and blushed at the newspaper boy who always winked at her.

Annie glanced in a store window. A few curls had escaped the braid and fell down her neck. Her large green eyes stared back from the reflection and she quickly looked away, quickening her step. She was determined to finish the last chapter of her book before Gemma got to the bridge.

As Annie walked along, she pulled her father's latest correspondence from her bag; she had an uncanny ability to walk and read at the same time. Where was her father on this fine day? She wondered. He never put down a return address but sometimes he would let things slip and she would know exactly where he was. Once, he admitted he was dining and listening to one of his favorite songs, "Revolution." She knew immediately he was in London at the Hard Rock Café.

The warm salutation greeted her at the opening of her father's letter. Annie smiled. Ethan Dibble was a drifter. What little money he made, he shared somewhat with his sister, Teresa. He had been a semi-successful newspaper man after college and was climbing the success ladder when his wife died. After that, his life wasn't stable enough to raise a daughter, so he gave Annie to his sister's care and showed up occasionally. And, it was never enough for Annie.

But, even so, living with Aunt Tess actually suited her. Her aunt didn't really care what she did or where she went. Annie could leave early on a summer's morning and not come home until long after nightfall. Aunt Tess was far too consumed with her work, her children, and her boyfriend to care what Annie was doing. That is, except when Ethan Dibble came with money and seeking a report on Annie's school marks.

Annie looked up. She was now almost at Wigan's Pier and she looked around for Gemma. Her friend was nowhere in sight, so Annie parked herself on the grass near the canal. She closed her eyes and took in a deep breath. It felt good to be alone for a few minutes. She stretched out on the luxurious lawn and decided to finish her father's letter.

". . . I've been able to catch a little work up north here and I'll be coming to see you and Tess next month in time for your birthday. Sixteen, is it? Cheers, my dear. Just give me time to save up some cash. Thanks for your patience—it means a lot to me."

Annie read her father's ramblings about a little writing he had been able to do. She guessed he was in Dover from the way he described his days. She longed to be with him in the north of England.

"Hey, Annie." Gemma's voice broke the stillness. Annie frowned when she saw the despair on her friend's face.

"What is it?" asked Annie.

"Lizzy is missing! Our whole neighborhood's been out searching, especially down at the river." Gemma plunked down beside Annie and buried her face in her hands. "I haven't slept for two nights."

"I hadn't heard—I'm so sorry."

"No trace of her anywhere—it's not like her to go off without a word." Tears trickled down Gemma's face and she wiped them with the back of her hand. "She had gotten in a fight with Mum and Dad but I didn't think she would be gone for more than an hour. Annie, what if . . ."

The unfinished sentence hung in the air like a rain cloud. Neither girl said a word as they watched the birds flit along the waterway and watched a young couple crossing Potter's Bridge. Leaves caught in the swirling eddies of the canal, spinning their way downstream.

"If I came up missing, no one would even notice," said Annie.

"Your dad would never give up looking."

"I suppose." Annie looked wistfully at the letter. No return address. No way to contact the one person in the world she cared the most about. He just came passing in and out of her life like a distant relative who just shows up for weddings and funerals. Tears burned her eyes and she looked away, upstream where a little barge was making its way down the canal.

"Mum wants me back right away. Had to talk fast to get her to let me come to tell you. Take care, Annie. I'll be in touch."

Gemma rose from the grass, gave Annie a hug and walked back over the bridge. Annie stood staring after her, thoughts swirling like the eddies in the canal. Lizzy two days missing? When would she see Gemma again?

Annie stooped to grab her book and shoved it into her handbag. She reached for her letter lying on the grass and when she stood again, she gasped. A man in a long, blue overcoat was suddenly standing over her. She had not even heard him approach.

"Might I have a moment of your time?"

"Why, of course," replied Annie.

Answering that simple question was the last thing Annie remembered on that summer day in August of 2016.

Three

Never in all her life had she seen anything so brilliant. It begged to be touched; but, as her hand reached upward, Annie Dibble realized she would have to be eight feet tall to even come close.

"Pretty, isn't it?"

Startled, Annie turned to the voice. A boy was sitting on a cot frame with a cushion on it. His dark hair was overdue for a cut, and he was nursing a wound just over his steel-gray eyes. The rag he held in his left hand was soaked in blood and he kept dabbing at the wound.

"What?" responded Annie. Her head was throbbing and she reached up to it, half expecting to feel that she, too, had a wound. But, she felt nothing. She looked around the room. Not only was the ceiling she had been staring at the most polished, gleaming silver she had ever seen, but it also made up the walls and all the furnishings. It dazzled her eyes and made her headache even worse.

"I said I think it's pretty—have you ever seen anything like it?" repeated the boy.

"Why, no, how could I? What is this place, anyway?" Annie frowned, frightened and confused.

"I haven't the slightest idea." The boy left the cot and went to the window. It was glazed over with opaque paint. "I woke up in this room just like you did; maybe an hour before—it's hard to say because I was just as foggy as you are." He leaned against the wall and gazed at a picture. It was of students in a classroom. All the students were dressed in plain, white uniforms. They all looked about fourteen years old, had the same hair color and haircuts, and sat with hands folded at simple wooden desks. The entire picture had a sterile look about it. And, not one of the students was smiling.

By now, Annie had swung her legs over the side of the cot. It was a twin to the one on which the boy was sitting. She let her hand slide down the leg of the frame and she found it to be silky, almost liquid to the touch.

"Uncanny, isn't it? I'll throw in *weird* and *eerie*, too." The boy was toying with a bracelet on his right wrist that seemed to be made of the same substance. He leaned on his cot until his back touched the wall.

Who was this boy, wondered Annie. His attitude seemed rather casual, especially in the face of what, to her, seemed a disturbing mystery.

"You've got one, too." The boy sat up straight and pointed to Annie's arm.

Her hand went straight to her arm where she discovered she had a bracelet identical to the boy's. Annie gasped, her mouth open. The band of silver was so light she had not even noticed it. She twirled it around her wrist and looked up.

"I daresay this is a frightening mystery," said Annie.

"Hey, you're a Brit, aren't you?" A large grin spread across the young man's face.

"Yes, I am, but . . . can you see anything outside that window?"

"Not really—it's a big blur. I've been trying for the last half hour."

The boy's gaze dropped to the enormous, floppy handbag that lay at Annie's feet "Say, you wouldn't have the 'kitchen sink' in there, would you? I sure am thirsty." He went over to a silver basin in the corner and turned the faucet knobs. Nothing came out. "Whoever's running this place is sure stingy with the rations. In fact, there haven't been any."

Annie looked down at her feet. There was her huge, cavernous handbag. She pulled it onto her lap and undid the fastener. Reaching inside, she withdrew one of the bottles of water she had put in that morning.

"Hey, I was just kidding," said the boy, still at the basin. In three strides he was hovering over Annie with his hand outstretched for the water. "May I?"

Annie lifted the bottle but stopped mid-way to his hand. "First, I *must* know your name."

"I'm Jack—Jack Flint."

"Nice to meet you. I'm Annie Dibble."

Jack took the bottle, opened it, and drank nearly the whole thing in one long gulp. Then, tipping the bottle, he soaked the blood-stained rag and dabbed it once again to his wound. "Annie Dibble. Sounds English."

"I thought we already had that established." Annie pulled open the top of her handbag to inspect the contents. She reached in, pulled out an apple and tossed it to Jack. His silver bracelet flashed as he caught it. "Whatever have you done to your head?"

"It's what happens when you try to escape this place—over there." Jack pointed to the doorway which led out to a dimly-lit corridor. "There's some kind of zapping ray or something." Jack dabbed again. "Anyway, I probably won't try that again."

"You are very good at stating the obvious,"

Jack nodded. "Hey, do you remember anything from when you disappeared?"

"I don't know. I—I . . ." Annie couldn't finish her sentence and her mind drew a complete blank as if hours or days had been completely wiped out of her memory. She had no point of reference until one thought returned to her. "Actually, there is one thing—a man. I saw a man in a long, blue overcoat. He asked me for a moment of my time and then—"

"I had just shot a moose," interrupted Jack. "And, I was cleaning up when a man dressed the same way came up to me at Sheriff Cooke's car. For a split second all I saw was what looked like a gold pocket watch in the palm of his hand. Really creepy and then—"

"And, then . . .?"

"I found myself here, just like you."

"Sheriff Cooke? You work for a sheriff?"

"Well, not exactly—on Friday nights there's not much to do where I come from. So, I volunteer sometimes to ride along with the sheriff and help out. I had just put down a moose that got hit on the highway."

"And, where *do* you come from?"

"I'm from Idaho, a place called Rattlesnake Wash." Jack smiled. "That's in America—a long ways from England. Just a farming community, nice summers and hard winters." Jack returned to his cot. "Where in England are you from? London?"

"No, indeed. It's called Wigan. I was just saying goodbye to a friend and was going to do some reading along the canal bank when this business began." Annie rose from the cot and approached the silver wall. "Fascinating." She touched the surface, drew her hand back suddenly and winced. "I believe you're right about the strange texture. Not entirely pleasant, is it?"

"Not *entirely*," said Jack, his eyebrows raised. "So, what do you do in Wigan, England?"

Annie rubbed her head, hoping the headache would leave her. "I attend school and live with my Aunt Tess. She's Dad's sister. She has four children and works hard to raise them on her own. My dad pays her to keep me there with her. He's employed most of the time and he writes me occasionally." Annie's face fell. "My aunt probably hasn't even missed me." Then, she looked up. "I wish I could live with my father, but he's so transient. It wouldn't work out very well." Annie sighed. "What about you?"

"Well, we live on a ranch and I have chores before school and after. Also, I have ten brothers and sisters." Jack looked up.

"How delightful," replied Annie. "But, however does your mother manage with so many?"

"Well, everyone pitches in. It's not always fun, but there's no excuse for being bored. I'm the oldest and that can be a pain sometimes. I'm always expected to be the responsible one. Maybe that's why I like going off with the sheriff."

"Someone has to be the oldest—I read somewhere that the oldest is almost always more accountable and dependable."

"That would be me."

Annie frowned again. "But, what about this place? Where do you think we are?"

Jack glanced thoughtfully toward the window and the strange picture. "I'm trying to figure it out, but it's hard." He nodded his head toward the picture on the wall. "Those kids don't look too happy. I just hope the people who run this place don't have plans for us to join them."

"What shall we do?"

"Just wait and watch, I guess." Jack scratched his head. "Believe me, I'm taking everything in."

Suddenly, there came a voice over a loudspeaker. The lights in the room brightened and both Annie and Jack jerked with a start.

"Attention. You will have access to the water facilities for exactly one hour. In that time, you will take care of any personal hygiene needs that are necessary. Failure to comply will result in severe penalties. Time start, 60 minutes and counting . . ."

Jack jumped from his cot and headed for what looked to be a bathroom door. "I've already found out these people mean business. I'll take thirty and you take thirty, okay?"

Annie nodded. She grabbed hold of her handbag and hugged it to herself, gaining what little comfort she could from the only thing familiar to her. What was this place? They had obviously been kidnapped, but by whom? Who was the man in the blue coat? She could think of no motive for random kidnappings. Especially, since Jack Flint wasn't from England. She smiled. He was definitely American—self-assured, aggressive and somewhat cocky.

Jack emerged from the bathroom twenty minutes later. His wet hair was combed back and his wound was cleaned.

"I don't think you took your share of the time," observed Annie, rising from the cot with her handbag.

"Wouldn't be good to be late. I have sisters—you'll need my ten-minute donation." He stepped to one side as Annie slipped past him without comment.

Jack returned to the foggy window and cupped his hands around his face to shield out the light, trying to peer through the cloudy glass. It wasn't completely obscured. He focused on one spot and thought he could make out several skyscrapers along a skyline. There wasn't a skyscraper within 300 miles of Teton County. He frowned. What would anyone want with two teenagers from opposite ends of the world? What was up with the mandatory showers and the strange, silver enclosure in which he found himself? Himself and this girl from England. She seemed a little uptight but it was a good sign that she could take his teasing. Besides, she had a well-stocked traveling bag.

Annie entered the room half an hour later. Her hair fell in a thick braid down her back. She still wore the cotton blouse and skirt but she had managed to smooth them almost as if they had been pressed. She raised her eyes to the loudspeaker. *"Four minutes and counting . . . three . . ."* She looked nervously at Jack.

"What's to happen to us when the time has expired?"

"We'll find out soon enough," replied Jack. He left the window and stood between Annie and the doorway, waiting. "I just know we need to find a way to get out of here."

Two more minutes passed when Jack could see someone approaching from the dim corridor. He could feel Annie drawing closer from behind. Jack watched as the figure emerged from the darkness. It was a tall young man about twenty years of age. He touched a lit panel on the side of the door frame which turned green. Jack assumed the young man had just disabled whatever had zapped him earlier.

As the young man walked through the doorway and into the room, Jack observed his every move. A long, slim weapon was slung by a black leather strap over his right shoulder. Jack had never seen anything like it but to him it resembled a very sleek AK-47. The young man wore a trim, black uniform with a round, gold insignia on the left breast pocket. Jack stared. He had seen the emblem before.

"I am Eli. You will follow me," the young man instructed. He spoke with an accent Jack did not recognize. They followed him into the richly carpeted hallway.

The overhead lighting lit up as they progressed and then extinguished as they passed. Jack glanced behind him where it remained darkened. "They know conservation here, I can tell you," he said to Annie.

"There will be no speaking," said Eli. The tone of his voice held a menacing authority. Jack and Annie glanced at each other and continued on. Eli led them down several corridors. Every few feet were paintings or photographs. Some were like the one Jack saw in their silver room. Nearly all were of large groups of people with grim expressions and with plain, sterile uniforms. Others were mottos written in beautiful calligraphy. As the lights brightened, Jack read one: "Unity and Solidarity for All." Then, it faded as the lights dimmed and they walked on.

Finally, they came to some elevators. Eli motioned for them to enter. The ride was silent and smooth. When the doors stopped, the digital display over the door read, '38th floor'. The doors opened and Eli led them into another plain, dimly-lit hallway. At the far end were huge double doors. Each was embossed with the same emblem Eli wore on his uniform. They were twenty feet away from the doors when two guards in black uniforms came seemingly out of nowhere. They asked Eli for a password and then stepped aside. The doors opened majestically, as if bidden by magic.

Jack and Annie stepped into the room beyond and were temporarily blinded by the dazzling light from a bank of windows which ran in a semi-circle from one end of the enormous room to the other. Even the high ceiling was partially glass and open to the sky, the brilliant sunshine illuminating the blood-red carpet.

Exotic artwork adorned the walls; gigantic oriental vases with tropical plants filled the corners, and a stuffed, charging African elephant took up the entire left portion of the massive room. Through the enormous expanse of windows, Annie could see a river below with skyscrapers in the background.

Jack scanned the room for any frame of reference—there was so much to look at, he felt overwhelmed. He took a deep breath and tried to focus; he was only interested in what this had to do with him. His instincts were geared toward finding out the reasons behind the events of this strange day. And, then he saw a man sitting at an ornate desk near the windows. The man was bent over as if he were writing a letter. Books were stacked on either side of him, and there was a huge bowl of plump and luscious-looking fruit on one of the stacks. It reminded Jack that he was still hungry.

Annie, too, saw the man at the desk, but he wasn't the first thing to draw her attention. Not far from the window, half inclined on an old-fashioned chaise was a young girl softly humming and playing some kind of stringed instrument. She wore a pastel-colored flowing gown and her long, dark hair was caught up from her shoulders with silver clips. Her skin was honey-golden and when her eyes met Annie's, she shook her head from side to side. Annie's eyebrows knit together in a puzzled expression. Then, her eyes widened with recognition. There was no mistaking that the girl was Lizzy, Gemma's missing sister.

Four

The man at the desk looked old, as the first thing to draw Jack's attention was his full head of thick, white hair. It was short and trimmed impeccably. He raised his eyes when the girl Lizzy stopped playing her music. He rose and walked around the corner of his desk. "Ah, I've been expecting you." The man didn't smile but motioned for Jack and Annie to be seated in two plush chairs nearby.

Annie pulled her bag from her shoulder and sat in the closest chair while Jack took the other. The old man was tall and his demeanor commanding; and, for a man of his age, he was incredibly slender and fit. The uniform he wore was exactly like Eli's except the insignia on the pocket was embroidered in rich scarlet instead of gold. His eyes were green and penetrating and his gaze made Annie look down at her lap.

"I am General Graff and I suspect that by now you must be quite hungry." He didn't wait for an answer but merely waved his hand toward Lizzy who immediately left the room through a side door by the elephant. "She will return momentarily with some nourishment." Annie didn't like the way his teeth showed through his fleshy lips.

"So, Jack, how is that head of yours feeling by now? An unfortunate occurrence, but not uncommon."

"How do you know my name? What is this place?" replied Jack.

"All in good time. I am not prepared at this moment to divulge the circumstances of your arrival. At least, not until we've had time to discuss your options."

At that moment, a different girl entered through the side door. She was dressed in the same black uniform and carried two trays of food which she set on the coffee table in front of Jack and Annie.

"Excellent. I hope you will enjoy the cuisine." General Graff motioned toward the food. "Go ahead and eat while I talk." He clasped his hands behind his back and walked slowly toward the windows. "Firstly, you may enjoy knowing that we overlook the East River in New York City. That much I can tell you. The room in which we find ourselves is that of the Secretary General of the Federation of Peace and Solidarity. You will notice the emblem on the west wall."

Jack had just stuffed his mouth with something that looked like tofu. He had tasted tofu once when on a vacation with his parents. He hated it then and he discovered he hated it now. He glanced at the emblem on the wall. It was two huge elliptical bands encircling an intricately carved outline of the earth. Emblazoned on the arch of the upper curve of the plaque were the words, "Federation of Peace and Solidarity." On the lower curve was a motto, *'Commune Bonum'*. Jack first saw that emblem the night he disappeared. It was on the pocket watch of the man with the blue coat. It was also on the pocket of everyone who worked in this place.

Jack pushed the tofu aside and bit into a gray piece of fish that looked as though it had been boiled too long. He looked around for some salt, but to no avail. The rest of the meal consisted of green salad and cooked spinach. Then, to his relief, he spied a large wheat dinner roll. He searched for butter, but there was none. Annie seemed content with the meal, eating in silence.

"Now, I couldn't help noticing the first impression Old Sadie made on you." The General pointed to the elephant. "A trophy I earned about five years ago on one of many expeditions into Tyrania. Deepest African jungles on earth, you know. Took a party of over a thousand to accomplish the journey. Lost a goodly number to disease and . . . well, discipline."

Jack took another bite of fish and let his eyes wander around the room as the General droned on. His eyes drifted to the massive emblem of the earth. On one side of the plaque was a beautiful painting of a rain forest and on the other was an ornate digital clock with the time and date. The time read *1030,* and the date read, August 13, 2036. Jack choked and reached for the glass of water on the tray.

"Are you all right?" asked Annie. She handed him the glass.

Jack nodded and continued coughing, barely able to get the water down. General Graff looked at Jack and then at the digital clock.

"Oh, he'll be all right. There are various reactions to finding oneself in a different time element. Unfortunately, when it occurs at mealtimes, it can be most annoying," said Graff. He walked over to the clock and straightened it. When he raised his arm, a silver bracelet glimmered, catching Annie's eye. When the clock was in her clear view, she gasped.

"No, Miss Dibble, your eyes do not betray you. The year is 2036, and, yes, you have been transported twenty years into your future. And, I suppose you would like to know why."

Annie was thankful that Jack had stopped coughing. This was some kind of bizarre trick—a bogus date on the clock for a purpose she couldn't begin to fathom. Whatever the circumstances, she was glad she was not alone. She looked at Jack and searched his eyes. He pushed the tray aside and leaned back in the chair.

"I don't know what your angle is, but just what is the point of bringing us here, General? We're just a couple of kids," said Jack.

"Very true, but I've been watching you carefully for the past few years. You have certain qualities that I feel I can incorporate into my program—qualities that I find lacking in my associates."

"Like what?" asked Jack. The man seemed deranged and Jack decided to humor him until he could figure out a plan to get out of there.

"Like fortitude, determination, and courage of conviction—and obedience. I've seen your organizational abilities, your competence under pressure, your resourcefulness—I need someone like you, Jack."

Graff then turned to address Annie. "And, as for you, Miss Dibble, you have an uncanny awareness of group psychology, an aptitude for group persuasion and a brilliant ability to convey it by the spoken and written word. Why, the other day, you almost convinced *me* of your political theories. Can you imagine?" He snorted and winced. "Nevertheless, I have great hopes you will be open to some, let us say *re-education.* I have some persuasive arguments of my own, you know."

"Arguments about what, General?" asked Annie, wondering how this man knew things about her that even *she* didn't know. His conversation seemed intelligent and completely insane at the same time. She looked at Jack who arched one eyebrow. She arched hers in return.

"Dear girl, there are many philosophies and points of view in the world—always have been. I just want to open your mind to a different way of looking at things. After all, if you look at the new society, you can't help but see the progress that's been made. The will of the collective whole has been achieved! Things previously thought impossible have come to pass and in just one or two generations! It will be my pleasure in the coming weeks and months to open to your view the many possibilities of my program. It's nothing like the past. You come from a dark era. Many programs deemed impossible a few decades ago are a part of everyday life now."

"What *kind* of new society?" asked Annie.

General Graff turned on his heel and strode over to the window. He stretched his arms wide. "There are so many accomplishments I wish to share with you. I—I hardly know where to begin. Why, the Institute of Re-Education, IRE, for example, has been responsible for the eradication of dissenting dialogue for the past ten years! That alone has given us the freedom to instigate cooperative controls and ease the confusion and uncertainty of millions."

"Sounds like the eradication of free speech to me," muttered Jack.

"Shh," said Annie.

"IRE has been responsible for rounding up the irritating rebels who always want to thwart programs which would benefit the common good. I'm proud to say that I personally was responsible, in my youth of course, for putting down over a thousand rebellions all around the world. Our military forces are unmatched as they've grown over the years. No one who lives within its borders dares to speak against the Federation. Of course, there are those bothersome pockets of dissent here and there, but my forces are always ready to crush them if they gain any strength to speak of." Graff hesitated. "How is your meal? I'm afraid I've rambled on terribly."

"Hmm," said Annie as she nodded her head and bit in to her dinner roll.

"Now, as I was saying . . . with the new liberal parameters enjoyed by the Department of Public Health and Utilities, conservation of natural resources has skyrocketed. Their brilliant water ration plan ensures that each individual has the opportunity of having the essentials of personal hygiene. I believe you witnessed that firsthand before you were brought to me this morning. Mandatory sanitation has been implemented in three-quarters of the world's population."

"What if you have a family of *twelve* who have exactly one hour to shower?" whispered Jack to Annie.

Annie waved her hand and shushed him again.

"And, then there is my personal favorite—the eradication of human obesity. We have the Global Obesity Prevention Program to thank for that. Evidence of their endeavors is apparent in the excellent meal provided this morning." Graff gestured toward the trays on the coffee table.

Jack sat forward in his chair, his fingers raking his hair. "That's fascinating, General. And, just how *do* you enforce healthy eating among the masses?" he asked, not trying to mask his sarcasm.

"Not a difficult question—regulation, pure and simple. Most populations have no trouble governing themselves at this point in time. Choices are limited and what we don't see, we don't think about, do we? It's a good plan and quite enforceable, I assure you. Obesity has been virtually eliminated in our society." Graff sat on the edge of his desk. "And, for those unwilling to cooperate, IRE has another arm which deals with insurgents—they soon learn it is better to cooperate than to go out on their own. In this modern world, there is no room for those old-fashioned, revolutionary ideas."

"I don't see what we have to do with all this," said Jack, frowning.

"I am surprised you haven't come to the same conclusion as I," stated Graff.

"And, what would that be?" asked Jack tonelessly. He felt darkness gathering in the room, like impending storm clouds. A tight feeling gripped him and made it hard to breath. Then, a vision of General Graff came into his mind—a raging, livid General Graff ready to strike Jack not just with his words but with the black baton fastened at his side to his shiny leather belt. Jack blinked and the vision disappeared. He forced himself to focus on the moment and waited for Graff's answer.

Graff walked over to the giant Federation symbol on the wall. His eyes widened. He looked demented. "This may just be a symbol, but it represents all that we have worked for! The motto '*Commune Bonum*'—Do you realize what that means? Jack, it means *for the common good*! My young people, we have accomplished programs that have leveled the playing field. Everyone is important in today's world—everyone!" Graff paused as if regrouping his thoughts. "Jack, I want you to be my right-hand man—my Deputy General. I know your talents. If you will serve me, I promise you worlds you cannot now comprehend."

"Look, General, I don't know where you're getting your information about me, but even if it was all true, I'm not interested in your program. And, frankly, the world I'm in is about all I can comprehend as it is. Now, if you don't mind . . ." Jack rose from the chair, ready to leave.

"I've seen what you can do with my own eyes!" shouted Graff. "You have no idea what you're capable of! I will have your obedience and I will have it willingly!" His eyes grew wild with rage and his fat lips widened in a deranged smirk. "I will have your compliance or I will have you *dead*!"

The vision from a moment before was coming true. Jack pulled Annie to the side and headed for the door. Behind him, General Graff had pulled the black baton from his belt and was raising it in the air when suddenly the double doors opened. Eli walked forward and bowed to General Graff.

'I am at your service, General," said Eli quietly.

The General, with baton still raised, stopped short. He glanced back and forth from Eli to Jack. Then, in an instant, Graff lowered his baton. He reached for a handkerchief and wiped his sweaty face. "Certainly, my good Eli." He was trembling. "I—I was just about to summon you. Take Mr. Flint and Miss Dibble back to their quarters immediately."

"Yes, sir." Eli turned to Jack and Annie and pointed to the open door. "You will proceed after me." The enormous doors swung silently shut, closing out the brilliant light from the room behind them.

"I think I made him mad," said Jack.

"He *is* mad! The man is mental! Psychotic!" Annie looked at Jack who was smiling. "Oh, you're joking! What a time for levity—he scares me to death!"

"Me, too. And, seriously, I think they may be ready to get rid of us. I probably shouldn't have spoken for both of us. I have a way of taking over sometimes," said Jack.

"You expressed my sentiments perfectly. I just want to go home!"

"Silence," ordered Eli.

Five

Jack Flint, Annie Dibble, and Eli continued the silent walk back to the holding cell. The lights brightened and then dimmed as they passed along the corridor. Jack was deep in thought, trying to come up with an escape plan. Slim chance that he could overpower Eli when he himself was weaponless and the young man had a rifle slung over his shoulder. And, he looked like he could use it.

In twenty feet, they would be at the elevator doors and Jack was desperately trying to figure out his next move when from the hallway to the left came another armed guard. He stopped to speak to Eli when suddenly Eli had the rifle off his shoulder. He swung the butt of his gun at the guard's head. The man fell to the floor in an unconscious heap. The doors of the elevator opened and three men pulled Jack and Annie inside. Eli threw the unconscious guard's gun to Jack. Remaining in the hallway, Eli stared at Jack. "I shall go another way," he said as the doors slowly closed.

Jack spun on his heel, facing the three men. "We can't just leave him!"

"We have our orders," said the one in front.

"I don't know who you are, but this is no kind of rescue in my book! If you want me, we go back!" Jack pointed the rifle at the leader.

"Put that thing down!" the man shouted. His chin was bristly with at least three days' growth of whiskers and his face was becoming beet red with rage.

"I don't know why you're here, but I'm not going to desert that guy!" yelled Jack. He thrust the gun menacingly in front of the leader's face. The leader clenched and unclenched his fists and ground his teeth with fury.

"All right, Flint, but this may be the last thing you ever do!"

"So be it," replied Jack. He pushed the button that opened the door, wondering how the man knew his name. The corridor was deserted except for the unconscious guard still lying on the floor. Eli was nowhere to be seen.

Jack turned to Annie. "I'm dead serious this time—Close these doors after we leave and don't let anyone in unless you know it's us!"

"But, how will I know if it's you?" Annie's voice was shaking.

Jack thought for a moment. "I'll say something only you would know like . . . like Rattlesnake Wash. Did you hear that, guys? It's Rattlesnake Wash if you want back in. Now, let's go!"

Annie watched through the closing elevator doors as the men disappeared into the darkened corridor. She slumped down onto the floor, drew her handbag to her and buried her face in her knees.

When they were outside the elevator doors, the leader, still visibly enraged, spoke. "All right, I'll take it from here, Flint. I'm Garcia and you'll do what I say." The man glared at Jack with hatred. "Now, listen up . . . Two go down to the right and two straight ahead. We double back in exactly five minutes if we haven't found that guy. Whoever makes it back—get on the elevator and head for the rendezvous point. It's too dangerous to wait." He frowned. "Klipstein you take Flint and go to the right. Move!"

The team split up and Jack and his partner crept down the hallway in front of the elevator on the right.

"Do you remember what that guy, Eli, looked like?" asked Jack.

"Yeah, I saw him."

The duo sneaked down the hallway until it turned to the left and continued scanning for Eli. A million thoughts were going through Jack's head. Why didn't Eli just jump on the elevator with them? Especially when he had just assaulted a Federation guard? The hallway remained empty. Jack was surprised they had encountered no one. That fact made him doubly nervous. Maybe the Federation forces were regrouping. Did they even know about the altercation at the elevator? Jack focused on every sound or movement.

Suddenly, Jack saw an image in his mind of the girl Lizzy running with Eli. He felt sure it was just around the next corner. In front of him, there was nothing and no one.

"Klipstein—they're around the next corner," whispered Jack.

"How do you know? You can see through walls?"

"I don't know *how;* I just know they're there." Jack began running toward the corner of the corridor and rounded the bend just in time to see Eli and Lizzy disappear through a doorway. "There they are!"

Jack and Klipstein ran to the doorway. Klipstein kept sentry while Jack gently knocked. "Eli, it's me, Jack. We've come to get you."

Silence.

"Eli, we're risking our skins for you—come out now!" said Jack frantically.

"Give him the password—Turtlebay!" said Klipstein.

"Password?"

"C'mon! Turtlebay—he's workin' for us!" There was an edge of panic in Klipstein's voice.

Jack pressed his mouth as close to the door as possible and said, "Turtlebay." Immediately, the door opened a crack. That was all Jack needed as he barged in, followed by Klipstein who quickly closed the door. Eli stood stiffly as if he were a wooden soldier when he saw the two men.

"You should not have come. I did not plan it this way. Go!" stated Eli.

"Not on your life," said Jack. "We're wasting time—two others are going to meet us back at the elevators and if we're not there, they're going to leave. Eli, I didn't come back here to die for you!"

Eli looked at the floor and then back at Jack. "Indeed not." He grabbed a small black satchel that he clipped to his belt and started toward the door, the others following.

"Wait a minute! Where's the girl you were with?" asked Jack.

"There are many secret exits in this building—she has gone. She was not seen aiding me. I believe she will be all right."

"Enough talkin'!" shouted Klipstein.

Eli quickly opened a desk drawer in the corner of the room and withdrew a handgun which he slipped inside his belt. Then, the three of them re-entered the passageway. There was no sign of anyone and that made Jack nervous. It had been too easy. This was no game of hide and seek and the stakes were infinitely higher.

They had passed the bend in the corridor and it was now just a short distance until they would be near the elevator hallway—around the next corner and it would come into sight. They could hear nothing, just the soft hum of the electric lights overhead as they brightened and dimmed. Jack thought his senses had never been so heightened, had never been so keen in anticipation of the moment.

They had just rounded the corner before the elevator and still there was no one. And then, suddenly, Jack heard a high-pitched whine that was completely foreign to him.

"Someone's shooting!" shouted Klipstein.

They ran to the elevator and stopped. Coming from the opposite direction were Garcia and the others and chasing them were at least four Federation guards. It was impossible to open fire without hitting Garcia and his men. And, Jack was reluctant to have Annie open the elevator doors at this point. They would just have to stand their ground.

"We'll cover you!" shouted Klipstein to the others. "Run!"

Immediately, the two men tore into a sprint in their direction. Shots from the guards rang out. Then, Eli took aim and picked one off. Klipstein opened fire on the guards. Encouraged, Jack hefted the sleek weapon Eli had thrown to him earlier and took aim. He focused and pulled the trigger, but it only clicked. Eli reached over and flicked a switch.

"Aim," Eli ordered.

Jack was surprised to find the gun so lightweight. Through the scope, the hallway was magnified and crystal clear. His heart skipped a beat. Re-enforcement guards were joining the original group. And, there were at least fifteen of them.

By now, Garcia's group had reached the elevator and had opened fire down the hallway. Eli and Jack were firing at will. But, for every guard Jack dropped, two took his place. Jack glanced around— they were sitting ducks. They fled to the opposite wall, out of the line of fire to regroup. They had to get into the elevator, but if Annie opened the door on Jack's cue, she would be fully exposed to the guards' gunfire.

"We've got no time! I'll give Annie the go-ahead and we go as a wall of fire!" Jack said as he met Garcia's hard stare. Garcia nodded.

"If we do nothing, we're dead anyway!" shouted one of the men.

"Okay, right after the doors open, we charge!" shouted Garcia.

Jack cupped his hands around his mouth and took a deep breath. "Rattlesnake Wash!"

In seconds, the elevator doors began to move.

"Now!" screamed Garcia.

All of the men moved into place in front of the elevator doors and opened fire. The whining of the AKS rifles reached a fever pitch. Several guards lay dead, scattered down the corridor. More were coming fast but hesitated when they saw the front Garcia and his men had created.

"Into the elevator!" yelled Garcia. The men tumbled through the open doors, still firing their weapons. Then, Klipstein groaned. Just as he crossed into the elevator, he collapsed.

Instantly, the elevator door closed. Garcia dragged the wounded Klipstein into the back where Annie cowered in the corner. Near the doors, Jack started to hit the 'down' button when Eli shoved him aside and hit the 'up' instead.

"Are you crazy?" shouted Jack. "We'll be trapped! They'll just be waiting for us if we go *up*!"

Eli said nothing but stood like a sentinel before the doors, holding his weapon across his chest. Jack could see that it was pointless to talk with him. He moved to where Annie was leaning against the wall, as the elevator rose. "Are you okay?" he asked.

"I'm trying to be," she answered. Her eyes filled with tears. "What is this horrible place? Everyone here is mad! Guns going off and people getting killed!" Annie backed tightly into the corner of the elevator as if that would give her comfort.

"I know," replied Jack. "It's all so bizarre." Jack watched the digital display which read off the floors. They hadn't gone far when it read, '40'. Garcia, standing by the doors, turned to address the others.

"Okay, we'll be at the rendezvous point three minutes after exiting. Parrish and I will clear the area. Flint, you and the girl stay glued to Klipstein. Skeen help them out." Then, he spoke directly to Jack. "And, if there's any more funny business, I'll take you out." Jack didn't doubt from the look on his face that he meant it. "Eli, you and Shane bring up the rear. Ready?"

All eyes were on Garcia and all heads nodded. Jack shouldered his gun on one side and grabbed Annie's arm. "Stay as close to me as you can." Annie's hands grasped his arm tightly and she nodded.

"Okay, let's go, Parrish," yelled Garcia as he pushed the elevator 'open' button.

Jack's heartbeat thundered in his ears and the adrenaline quickened his senses. Annie's fingers dug into his flesh.

Garcia and Parrish were immediately out the door and scanning for the enemy with their weapons ready. Garcia motioned for the others to stay put. They ran forward and ducked behind a wall. When the scene was quiet for a few moments, he gave the others the 'thumbs up'.

Jack and Annie followed Skeen who was aiding Klipstein. He limped severely and blood had soaked his pant leg. Nevertheless, he readied his gun in anticipation of the Federation guards.

Garcia motioned for the group to follow him up a flight of metal stairs. Eli and Shane were watching the rear as they all fled upwards to a large cement helipad. Garcia led them to an enclosure for protection.

"How're you doing, Klipstein?" Garcia addressed the wounded man.

"Okay—I just hate that I'm slowin' you down," he said with a wince.

"Listen up! Parrish and I will take the lead. Skeen, you and Flint get Klipstein aboard— everyone else follow! Eli and Shane—you bring up the rear. Understood?"

Everyone nodded again. Annie turned to Jack and whispered, "Aboard what?"

"A helicopter of some kind." Jack bit his lip. "Not like one *I've* ever seen."

"How do you know?" asked Annie.

"Been seeing it in my mind for the past twenty minutes," answered Jack with a sheepish look on his face. Then, suddenly in the distance came a sound like a thousand drums beating in unison. High in the sky came a huge black helicopter, its rotors pulsating as it began its long descent.

"I'll be right back," said Jack as he sprinted over to Garcia.

"Garcia, I know you have no use for me, but you've got to believe me—a group of guards is going to rush us when we get halfway to the helicopter. Leave me in position and I can pick 'em off."

"Look, kid, that stunt back in the elevator tells me all I need to know about you. Now, get back with Klipstein and shut up!" yelled Garcia. The man looked ready to strangle him. Jack knew there was no use convincing him of the picture that had just come into his mind. He looked around, not knowing what to do. Then, he ran to where Eli and Shane were posted.

"Eli! We're about to be ambushed! Garcia won't listen to me! I don't know where this is coming from but—"

Eli's hand went up to silence Jack. "You have a time signature. Garcia should know this." His face clouded over. "Flee with the others. Shane and I will cover for you." His dark eyes bored into Jack. "You will do as I say."

"Right," said Jack. As he ran toward Annie, his eyes rose to the incredible black machine which now hovered over the 'X' on the landing pad. It had two large turbine-looking engines and short wings in addition to the rotors that were slicing the air. Jack had never seen anything like it.

"Okay, run for it!" shouted Garcia.

Klipstein hobbled with Skeen holding his arm, followed by Jack and Annie, her huge bag flopping at her side. Then, Jack rushed ahead, slung Skeen's other arm over his shoulder and the two men flew up the ramp that had materialized as the helicopter touched the tarmac. Then, the whirring sound of gunfire filled the air. Jack returned for Annie, picked her up and practically threw her into the interior of the helicopter.

Jack realized that the ambush had begun. He looked at Garcia who scowled and ordered him into the helicopter. "You've done your part, now get back!" Garcia shouted.

Jack ducked into the helicopter and collapsed onto the floor in exhaustion. Everyone inside could hear the intense gunfire. Garcia crouched near the doorway with his weapon ready. "Where are they?" he shouted. A minute passed, the gunfire never letting up. Sweat poured down Garcia's face, as he grit his teeth and swore. "I'm going back and—" He stopped. It was suddenly silent outside.

Garcia turned to his men. "Get ready for anything!" He and all the men rose to their feet, aiming their weapons and preparing to exit. Garcia had just taken a step when Eli came up the ramp dragging Shane who was completely limp.

"Get us out of here!" yelled Garcia to the pilots.

Eli laid Shane on the floor and slumped down, hovering over Shane's silent form.

"Lift off!" shouted Garcia as the huge automatic doors closed, locking with a solid clank. Immediately, the machine began to rise.

The powerful upward surge made Jack's stomach lurch and his arms flail to find some support. He glanced forward and saw Annie strapped into her seat staring at him. He arched his eyebrow. She managed a weak smile and did the same.

"What's that clinking sound?" asked Jack.

"They're still firing at us," answered Skeen. "You'd think they'd learn—they can't penetrate the outside of this thing." He looked at Jack and pointed to one of the many seats that lined the wall of the aircraft. "Better strap yourself in."

Jack pulled himself up and into one of the seats and marveled that it was made of rich, black leather. He glanced around the interior. Everything inside the helicopter was expensive and luxurious, from the overhead lighting to the black, plush carpeting. It didn't seem like a military helicopter at all.

"Nice, huh?" commented Skeen. "Only the best for Com Two."

"Com Two?" asked Jack.

"Yeah, Commander Two. He spared no expense with this baby."

Jack took a moment to gaze around at the furnishings in the aircraft. His heart was just beginning to calm into a steady rhythm when his eyes fell to Annie. She was leaning back in her seat with her eyes closed. He figured she was trying to block out the strange horror of the day. He glanced at the rescue crew, all in khaki uniforms, and sitting alert. Strangely, they were all staring at him. One by one, they looked away, but whenever Jack raised his eyes, their stares returned.

Jack looked out the window. The aircraft was now far above the helipad and heading straight up. It banked to the left and then Jack saw it. They were pulling away from a building he had seen many times in his school books. Fading now in the distance was the unmistakable outline of the United Nations building. They were now high above a river, undoubtedly the East River, as General Graff had said.

Garcia leaned forward in his seat, his arms across his knees. "What d'ya think, Doc—is he gonna be all right?"

Parrish was bent over Shane with an open medical bag. He shook his head, his eyes full of sorrow. "I'm sorry, Captain."

A hush fell over the men as the news quietly spread. Garcia hit the wall with his fist and swore, his eyes slowly burning into Jack.

Then, the pilot's voice came over the loudspeaker. "Passengers please see that you are secured in your seats. That goes for you, Doc. Preparing for flight transformation in three." Immediately, the pilot and co-pilot began pushing buttons and levers. Overhead lights brightened and a metal plate began covering the windows. Parrish left the dead man and secured himself and Klipstein in seats near the back. In the promised three minutes, the plane surged forward with the power of a jet plane. Jack gripped the arms of his seat and glanced at Annie. Her eyes as well as her mouth were wide open.

"What *is* this thing," Jack mumbled under his breath.

"It's a heliplane. We're going to see Com Two, on his orders," said the man next to him. He was in a dark green uniform with a star insignia on the pocket.

"So, do you know where we're going?"

"Base camp," the man replied.

"Where's that? Washington?" asked Jack.

"They'll tell you when we get there. Best be getting some rest, after what you've been through." The man leaned back in his seat and crossed his arms, pushing his cap over his eyes.

"Hey, one more question," ventured Jack. "If there's a Commander Two, who's Commander One?"

The man raised the brim of his cap, fixed his eyes on Jack and smiled wryly. "Well, I guess you'll be finding out soon enough." He pushed his cap back down over his eyes. "It's you, kid—you're Commander One."

Six

Two hours had passed after Jack drifted off to sleep, his head leaning against the black leather seat of the heliplane. A shift in altitude must have woken him. He rubbed his eyes and face awake and stretched.

Jack turned his head to see Annie in her seat near the front of the plane. She was reading and didn't look up. Immediately, Jack's thoughts turned to Shane. The man's body had been moved sometime after the jet surge of the aircraft. Jack felt a heavy depression. If only Garcia had listened to him, they could have been better prepared for the ambush. As it was, there was no one to back up Eli and Shane. Somehow, Jack knew Garcia would blame the entire incident on him.

"Attention, passengers. Prepare for landing in approximately twenty minutes."

Jack leaned forward and raked his fingers through his hair. How long had he been sleeping? His arm brushed a bottle of water in the drink holder of the seat. He didn't know who had put it there but he opened it and drank it all without stopping.

As he returned the bottle to the holder, he caught a glimpse of the silver bracelet around his right wrist. He had hardly had a moment to look at it at Federation Headquarters. There were absolutely no markings of any kind on it. It seemed to be made of the same material as the walls and furniture in the holding cell and he didn't particularly like the feel of it. He glanced at Annie. She had one and even General Graff. When the General brandished the baton from his belt, Jack had seen the flash of silver from Graff's arm. What could the silver bracelets mean and why did it seem everyone had one?

Jack looked up. Several men again were staring at him with great curiosity. They looked away in embarrassment. He knew he and Annie were the objects of the rescue, but why the stares? And, he discovered one thing about the guy sitting next to him—he had a weird sense of humor. If he thought it was funny to call Jack 'Com One,' it was a really cheesy joke.

Fifteen minutes passed when the plane began slowing down and the sound of the engines grew louder. The metal plates covering the windows slowly retracted and the beating of the rotors returned.

"Prepare to disembark in three minutes." The pilot's voice came over the loudspeaker.

Jack would have gathered his belongings, but he had none. He noticed that Eli still had his satchel but he had unfastened it from his belt and held it in his hands. He looked at Jack but did not smile.

The heliplane descended to a soft landing and the pilot cut the engines. The passengers walked single file down the ramp to the tarmac. Jack watched as Shane's body was carried respectfully off the aircraft. The other Coalition members removed their caps and saluted. Several, including the limping Klipstein, followed the stretcher off the tarmac.

Jack stood alone, his head hanging. Then, he watched Annie emerge from the heliplane. Her dark blonde hair was out of its braid and fell over her shoulders. She looked refreshed from the short rest, her eyes bright and searching. When she saw Jack, she went immediately to his side and slung her handbag over her shoulder. "So terrible about Shane."

"I somehow feel responsible."

"Certainly not. Why?"

"I saw it coming. I just couldn't get anyone to listen to me."

Annie shook her head sadly. "Just another part of this horrible day."

"Cut the chatter!" yelled Garcia, "We're coming into Security."

"I daresay he is taking this vendetta a bit too far," whispered Annie. "Not all of it was your fault."

"Yeah, just the part where Shane dies," Jack whispered back. "At least, that's what Garcia will think."

The large gray building they were approaching was modern in architecture and would have been unremarkable except for large metallic letters spelling out 'Pole Star' above the main entrance. To the right of the words was a slim diamond-shaped star. Mountains hung like a backdrop to the west where the late afternoon sun was casting long, golden beams into the clouds. Jack had the feeling that they were up high, as if on a mountaintop. But, for the moment he concentrated on filing through the double doors of what Garcia had described as 'Security.'

Guards wearing khaki-colored uniforms lined the entryway. The patches on their pockets had the same star design as the motif on the building. They were directed forward where a barricade of beautiful pine woodwork barred the way of going any farther. Several guards stood sentry beyond the barricade where there was a spacious, richly-furnished room that would have rivaled any four-star hotel lobby.

Most of the men who had been on the heliplane departed down other hallways until only Jack, Annie, Eli, and Garcia remained. Parrish had accompanied the body and Klipstein to the medical area as soon as they had arrived. As they waited, a woman in uniform appeared and crossed the enormous lobby beyond the barricade. She walked through a security door, stopped and then saluted Garcia.

"Good morning, Capt. Garcia. I can take it from here." The woman had a crisp, military bearing. She was slim and attractive and her auburn hair was swept back from her face in a neat bun. She smiled at Jack and Annie. "Welcome to Pole Star Base. My name is Lt. Shaw. If you'll please follow me."

Jack looked at Garcia, but Garcia only saluted Lt. Shaw, turned sharply on his heel and left in stony silence. Annie pulled on Jack's arm. "Let's go," she whispered.

Lt. Shaw led them through the security door and across the plush carpet of the elegant waiting room. They boarded an elevator at the far end of the room where Lt. Shaw clasped her hands behind her back for the wait. "How did you enjoy the flight?" she asked.

Jack cleared his throat. "Hey, we have about a million questions, starting with 'where in the heck are we'? We don't—"

"All of your questions will be answered momentarily. I appreciate your patience," answered the lieutenant. The elevator doors opened and they emerged and continued following Lt. Shaw.

Photographs lined the hallway on both sides. Most were scenes of military personnel with all kinds of aircraft. The pictures were of events completely foreign to Jack until they got to one at the end of the corridor. It was a picture of the Twin Towers in New York City moments after the second airplane had hit. Jack had seen that image many times. On the lower edge of the frame was the inscription, 'We Will Never Forget.'

Lt. Shaw approached an office door and knocked. "Just a moment." She opened the door a small crack. "Sir, they're here." Jack could barely hear a muffled reply from within the room beyond. Then, Lt. Shaw opened the door wide and motioned for them to enter. "I'll come back a little later," she replied.

Jack entered the office first with Annie close behind. The room was furnished conservatively. Filing cabinets were near some chairs to the left, a painting hung on one wall, and a large desk was by a row of windows. A man stood staring out the windows, his hands clenching and unclenching. When he turned to face them, the evening shadow obscured his face. "I'm so grateful you made it through this day safely—so very grateful." He slowly walked toward them until the light of the only lamp lit up his face.

Annie gasped. Her hand flew to her mouth. "Dad?" Her handbag fell from her shoulder as she ran to the other end of the room and into the man's waiting arms.

Annie clung to the man, her shoulders heaving in great sobs. "Oh, Dad, where are we? This has been the most horrible day of my life!" She continued to sob as the man gently patted her shoulder.

Jack still stood at the office doorway. He frowned as the strange scene played out before him. This was certainly not what he had expected. Apparently, this British girl he had known for less than a day had some secrets she wasn't sharing.

Regaining her composure, Annie pulled away and wiped her tears on her sleeve. She looked up at the man. Her face fell. "Dad, what's the matter? What's happened to you?"

The man looked down at her. "Annie, just a moment. Everything will be all right." He crossed the room and extended his hand to Jack. "Hello, Jack. I'm so very pleased you made it safely to Pole Star. Allow me to introduce myself—I am Ethan Dibble, Commander Two of the Coalition of Liberty."

"Thanks, sir," replied Jack.

Dibble was neatly dressed in the plain dark green uniform of the Coalition. He, too, had a badge on his chest with the star symbol and the letters C.O.L. His hair was thick and graying at the temples. The lines in his face added to his obvious concern.

"Please—Jack, Annie—be seated." Dibble motioned for them to be seated in two chairs in front of his desk. He sat and clasped his hands on top of the desk and gazed into Annie's eyes. "Annie, what you must be thinking!" Tears welled up in his eyes and he shook his head. He looked as though he had been up for days.

"I don't understand," replied Annie. "What's happened to you?"

"I don't know what they told you over at the Federation." He stopped. "I think I had better be quite candid here—they have fed you a whole lot of lies and propaganda."

"Indeed, they have," complained Annie. "We were forced to listen to their commander, a General Graff. He was ranting and raving like a madman. Oh, Dad, the man is delusional! Talking of bringing us up from the past and ridiculous things like—"

"Annie," interrupted Dibble. "That part wasn't delusional." He shifted in his seat. "That much is true." Dibble turned to his computer screen and typed something on the keyboard. "Look." He turned the screen on its swivel base so both Jack and Annie could see it. It was a newspaper headline. On the third line down, they read the date— August 13, 2036. "This is today's London Times."

Jack looked at the floor. Annie stared at her father, her mouth open.

"No! This can't be! There's no such thing!" Annie rose from the chair and grabbed her bag. She dug inside and pulled out two bagels. "I just put these in here—this morning. I was headed for Wigan's Pier ... met Gemma ... her sister missing..." Her sentence evaporated in the silence.

"Annie, sit down," said Dibble quietly.

Annie returned to her chair and stared at her father. "And, you have *aged* twenty years? Is that what you're telling me?" Annie felt light-headed, as though the room were spinning. "This cannot be," she said in a quiet whisper.

"Sir, time travel?" Jack shook his head. "It's hard to grasp, you know? I ... I..."

"Naturally, I don't expect you to comprehend everything at once. This day has been incredibly stressful for the two of you. Would you like to take a rest, perhaps talk some more after dinner? Maybe tomorrow?"

"There's no way I can function without knowing what's going on, sir. You can continue as far as I'm concerned," said Jack. He looked at Annie.

With a look of defeat, Annie nodded her head.

"Well, all right. Let me see—"

"Does all this have anything to do with a man in a long blue coat?" blurted Jack.

"Finke," stated Dibble. "His name is Finke."

38

"He carried a gold pocket watch in his hand. I saw it just about the time—"

"Chronomium."

Jack stared at Dibble, eyebrows raised, and looking perplexed.

"Chronomium was discovered seven years ago in '29." Dibble got up from his desk. "By a British chap named Wycliffe." He walked to the windows. "Very top secret stuff, you know. But, the way the world government is, it was just a matter of time until it came under the control of the Federation."

"Sir, just what *is* the Federation?" asked Jack.

"Dictatorship, my boy, plain and simple. The Federation of Peace and Solidarity! There *is* no peace and the only solidarity is the iron fist by which we are all ruled. Our dictator-in-chief, that self-proclaimed 'general' Graff—he's a fool. I've met the man on many occasions. . . yes, a fool . . .and we're stuck with him. That is why you and I evolved into the leaders of this movement." He turned from the window and looked at Jack. "Am I going too fast?"

"Not too fast, just too confusing. When you said *you and I*—that's where I got lost," replied Jack.

"Jack, in the past twenty years, you have risen from an obscure farm boy to leader of the foremost resistance movement in the world." He stopped. "I'll let you digest that for a moment." Dibble rang a bell on his desk. A girl in uniform appeared. "Please be so kind as to bring us some refreshments, Sgt. Thank you."

"How could that be?" asked Jack.

"Intolerance, Jack. It was the same for me. As world events evolved into something terribly ugly, I saw that I was wasting my life, my talents. I had been a drifter, avoiding my responsibilities." He glanced at Annie. "And, my daughter."

"What happened to you, Dad? I hardly ever saw you."

"I had to put the past behind me, Annie—forget the pain of losing your mother and do something worthwhile. The resistance movement was growing and I wanted to be a part of it, like you."

"Like me?"

"Annie, you are the leading voice of Radio Free America. You broadcast your message of freedom every day of the week over the airwaves—you are the hope of oppressed millions!"

"And how long have I been doing this?" Annie looked skeptical.

Dibble raised his head, searching his memory. "Let's see, you graduated from Oxford and then began writing for the London Times. You did a little broadcasting for the BBC. Then, FOPS took control of everything they could get their hands on. Eventually, Radio Free America was born and you pretty much worked your way to the top—with a little bit of help from me," he added with a smile.

"I can't believe it. Mostly, I just like to read," replied Annie.

"That's where it begins." Dibble turned to Jack.

"I'll be direct, Jack—we met over fifteen years ago. We were recruited into this movement by a friend. We both had our talents and brains and this is where it has all led to—the Coalition of Liberty. Rebel Base Pole Star in the mountain peaks of Norway. Commander One and Two. It is a powerful organization, very large, and recruiting more every day."

"How big is it?" Jack bit his lip. The enormity of what Dibble said was beginning to sink in.

"It is found in every nation on earth. People are searching—they want answers—they want the truth." He touched the badge on his uniform pocket. "This symbol represents just that. The star is Polaris, the Pole Star, always pointing north, sure and trustworthy. Just like the truth."

Jack leaned forward. "I can see why I was drawn to it. Whew! What crazy events have taken place just since I was a kid!" Then, he frowned and looked at Dibble. "But, I *am* a kid. I don't have twenty years' experience behind me and neither does Annie."

Dibble grew pale and grave and began wringing his hands. "I know. I've been contemplating that all day." He slowly walked closer to Jack and Annie. "This won't be easy to comprehend. In fact, I'm struggling with it myself." He raked his fingers through his hair. "The *first* thing I learned this morning was that you had both been timesnatched."

Jack cleared his throat. "Can't you just send us back?"

"No, because there's something else."

"What is it, Dad?"

Ethan Dibble's voice was raspy when he answered. "I can't send you back where you came from because . . . because the second thing I learned today was that Jack Flint and Annie Dibble have both been killed."

Seven

The sun had set at Coalition Base Pole Star and there was a light on high in the office of Com Two. He sat sipping a glass of wine as he watched two teenagers dine on steak and lobster.

"Never had lobster," said Jack as he stuffed his mouth. He buttered a dinner roll and dove into a large helping of noodles with cream sauce. "Where did all this food come from? General Graff said it had all been abolished."

"The idiot is drunk with power—thinks he controls the entire planet." Dibble snorted in disgust. "He finds it quite irksome that there are freedom factions worldwide, disturbing his dream of total world domination. Food such as you are eating is to be had in many spots of the earth. But, it does come at a price."

Annie dabbed her mouth with her napkin. "Getting back to what you said a little while ago—whatever do you mean that Jack and I were killed? Obviously, we are *not* dead." She took a sip of a sweet drink she had never tasted before.

"Precisely. But, we have had most of the day to analyze the reports. It would seem that the 2036 version of yourselves were both killed in a terrorist attack in Israel this very day. It is intricately connected with the timesnatching. You see, you cannot exist with your 'future selves' in the same time plane and proximity, so to speak."

"So where do we go from here?"

"I have my team of experts working on it now. We'll give them some time to come up with a plan. There's too much at stake to do anything rash." He knelt beside Annie and drew her to him. "Annie, I know this is so much to take in. Get a good night's rest and we'll see each other in the morning. The sergeant will show you both to your quarters." He rose to leave. "Oh, I nearly forgot—there is someone who would like to see you both." Dibble opened the door to his office. "You may come in now."

The door opened wider and Eli walked in. "Thank you, Commander. I shall only be a moment." Dibble left as he shut the door and Eli stood facing Jack and Annie. "I would like to explain some of my behavior of this day. May I sit down?"

Annie pointed to a chair nearby. "Yes, please join us." She watched Eli as he took his seat. He no longer wore the Federation uniform but had changed into the dark green of the Coalition. He was well-built and tall with dark hair that was trimmed in military fashion. His dark eyes looked up at Annie.

"I feel that some of my actions have caused you great difficulty, Com One."

"Just call me Jack."

"That would be utterly impossible, Com One."

"Why?"

"I have known you for several years by that title." Eli shifted nervously in his seat.

Jack glanced at Annie who raised her eyebrows.

"Does that look mean you're staying out of this?" he asked her.

Annie smiled.

Jack turned to Eli. "I think that among peers, especially since I'm not Com One yet, it's all right to call one another by first names."

"I am honored to be considered a peer."

"More than a peer, Eli. What do you call someone who saves your life?"

Eli didn't answer.

"How about we compromise and you just call me Flint?"

Eli looked down at his hands, deep in thought. "This seems important to you. I will concede."

"Thanks, Eli. Now what did you want to talk about?"

"I should never have retreated from the rescue. It caused you to rebel against Capt. Garcia. The original plan was to join you all in the escape. I had been working undercover for several months at FOPS headquarters. The infiltration had proved fruitful."

"Why didn't you obey orders?" asked Jack.

"I fully intended to carry out the operation as planned. That is until . . ." Eli fidgeted. "Until I met someone."

"Met someone?" asked Annie.

"The young girl you saw in the General's office—her name is Lizzy."

"I know—she's my best friend's sister. Eli, she was timesnatched just a few days before I was."

"Indeed. She is one of the timesnatched children living there at the headquarters building in New York." Eli sighed. "And, so by disobeying orders, I caused you to react with impunity which has greatly angered Capt. Garcia. He reacts to you now with great animosity."

"And, *loathing*—especially since Shane didn't make it," said Jack, his head down.

"If Capt. Garcia had heeded your warning, Shane's death may have been averted," said Eli.

"Maybe so, but Garcia won't look at it that way." Jack scratched his chin and sighed. "Are you going to be punished for what happened?"

"I have been justly reprimanded," answered Eli.

Annie interrupted. "Eli, why are they kidnapping children from the past?" she asked.

"In some instances, I am not sure. But, I do know that the general and the Prime Committee abduct individuals from the past that are a danger to him in the present day. That would be the case with the two of you. Com One—I mean, Flint—you were just such a person. And, Miss Dibble, you were also brought to the present in an effort to prevent your great success against him."

"This is unbelievable," said Annie. "Why was . . . am . . . I such a threat against him?"

"You underestimate yourself greatly, miss. Your voice comes over the radio waves in America and reinforces the freedom fighters. And, not just in America, but all over your world."

"So, you became fond of Lizzy?" asked Annie, pushing her hair from her eyes.

"Yes. I had hoped to bring her with us, but the timing was not right. I do not believe her life is in danger but I intend to return for her before my departure from the Coalition." Eli looked at both Jack and Annie with determination in his eyes.

"You'll be leaving the Coalition?" asked Jack.

"There is something I must explain. It will not be easy for you to believe it. But, I assure you it is true." Eli paused and straightened in his seat. "I am not from here."

"That's okay, neither am I." Jack's eyes narrowed. "So, you're not Norwegian—what does that matter?"

"No, you misunderstand me." Eli shifted in his seat, pursing his lips. "I was not born here; I mean, I am not from this earth."

Jack's eyebrows knit. He glanced at Annie whose mouth was a thin line. She was staring at Eli as if he had just told her she had two heads.

"So, what are you telling us, Eli? That you're from a different planet? That you're an alien?" asked Jack.

"Yes."

Jack slammed his fist on the desk. "That's about as easy to believe as us going twenty years into the future! C'mon what's next?"

"Jack," said Annie in a pleading tone, "Please."

"Flint, if you know nothing else about me, I would have you know this one fact; I would never lie to you. About three years ago, my intergalactic craft left me here on a sort of mission. The purpose was to integrate with the civilizations, to learn as much as I could and then return to my home base."

Jack continued staring at Eli incredulously. "I guess I shouldn't have shouted." Jack began pacing in front of Com Two's desk. "But, it's just that in *one day* I've been expected to believe the unbelievable." He shook his head and sighed. "Just give me some time."

Annie rose from her chair and stood by Eli's side. "How is it that you, if you're from another planet, I mean, how is it that you look like us?" asked Annie calmly.

"A very reasonable question," answered Eli. "It is a consistency that has intrigued my people for generations. There are many universal consistencies of this nature. I would like to tell you about them if time permits; that is, in the future, of course." Eli unclipped a small bag from his belt. It was the same one Jack had seen Eli attach to his belt during the rescue. "Perhaps it would help to see something from my world." He reached inside the bag and pulled out a small, round, furry ball.

Annie's eyes grew wide. Then, the ball in the palm of Eli's hand suddenly popped eyes, then a small stubby tail, and then four tiny paws emerged. The eyes were big and brown with thick black lashes. Floppy ears wiggled from side to side and the little animal stood on Eli's hand and stretched.

"What on earth?" whispered Annie. She reached out. Eli gently dropped it into her hand. The little animal gave a squeak and rubbed its tiny nose into her palm. Annie brought it up to her face and gazed into its enormous eyes. "What is it?"

"She is an arphax. Her name is Timna."

Jack walked to the Commander's desk and back, still taking in Eli's revelation. It was all so hard to comprehend. He was just beginning to grasp what Dibble had revealed and now Eli was taking them down another road. Eli had stated the preposterous, simply and matter-of-factly—and without apology. He looked at Eli watching Annie playing with the little creature. Then, he didn't know why, but somehow Jack knew that Eli was not capable of lying. As fantastic as Eli's story was, he felt himself giving in to it, comprehending that it was true. He gazed at Eli's pet called Timna and almost smiled. Eli's story had to be true—he had a little fur ball to prove it.

"I know this is difficult for you, Flint," said Eli.

"I believe you," responded Jack solemnly. "What choice do I have?" He patted Eli on the back. "Actually, the important thing I care about is that you saved Annie and me this morning—we'll always be grateful for that."

Annie turned to Eli. "I believe you, too, Eli." She stroked the little creature's head and reluctantly returned her to her owner. "But, Eli, what about Lizzy? How can you possibly go back?"

"The Coalition Council is going over the reports, as Com Two indicated. I have asked them to consider my request to rescue Lizzy."

Annie frowned.

"What is the matter, Miss Dibble?" asked Eli.

"They're not going to give you permission, Eli. I have this crazy feeling about it that I can't base on anything, really."

"You may have a time signature as well. Traveling through time sometimes endows the individual with a sort of 'sixth sense' as your culture would define it."

"Eli, Dibble didn't tell us much about time travel. I think he said it was discovered about seven years ago by a guy named Wycliffe. Can you tell us anything more?" asked Jack.

"I know very little, but I will share. The name Nicolas Wycliffe is known in few circles. When his discovery came to light, there was great fear it would become yet another weapon in the FOPS arsenal. And, unfortunately, that is exactly what occurred."

"How does a pocket watch let you travel in time?" asked Jack.

Eli set Timna in his lap and tickled her ear. She made a tiny squeak and looked up at her master. "The chronometer is not gold but an element known as chronomium. Though it looks and feels like gold, it obviously has properties above and beyond. The known reserves of the time metal have all been confiscated by the Federation. That is, with the exception of a small quantity held in reserve by the Coalition." He looked down at Timna as she rolled over in his hand.

"Can you explain these silver bracelets? Even General Graff had one," asked Annie.

"He's going to tell you it's not silver," said Jack.

"Shh."

"You are correct, Flint. It is called bohrium. It has been said that the inventor Wycliffe had a most unfortunate time travel experience. When he returned to his present day, he worked weeks around the clock in order to find an element that would counter chronomium. The element bohrium is the result of his research. It is Graff's way of keeping you here in your future. Indeed, the holding cell in which you found yourselves is lined with it so that you could not be sent back. He wears a bracelet as a defense against anyone attempting to abduct him out of his own time."

A knock came at the office door and Ethan Dibble stepped inside. "I saw the light still on."

"I beg your pardon, Com Two. It is my fault that I keep Flint and Miss Dibble from retiring."

"Nonsense," said Jack. "We've been firing questions at him non-stop, Commander."

"That is none of my concern," said Dibble. "I do have some information for you, though. I have no doubt that you've learned a few things from Eli here, so I hope this will make sense." Dibble put his arm on Annie's shoulder. "It's a fact that Jack Flint and Annie Dibble were together, at an Israeli café in Tel Aviv. A terrorist bomb blew up the café. Ten people were killed, including Com One and Miss Dibble."

Annie's face blanched. Her eyes grew wide as she saw that her father wasn't finished. Dibble had turned to face Jack.

"The Coalition Council has given permission for you and Annie to go to Tel Aviv to rescue them."

Jack felt as though he had just been ordered to reverse gravity. He glanced at Annie. "Rescue them?" he asked incredulously. "H—how do you rescue someone who's already dead?"

Commander Dibble walked across the room where Jack was standing. He reached forward, took Jack's hand and placed something in it.

Jack looked down. In the palm of his hand was a golden chronometer. On it was the emblem of a diamond-shaped star. Into Jack's mind came Com Two's words of a few hours before— '*It stands for Polaris, the Pole Star, always pointing north, sure and trustworthy. Just like the truth.*

Eight

Jack woke the next morning to the sound of yelling below his window. He opened the balcony door and walked into the warm sunshine. Below him were several hundred troops on a parade ground marching in the dark green uniform of the Coalition of Liberty. The balcony was high enough to see beyond the parade ground and to the magnificent mountains he had seen only briefly the afternoon before.

Coalition Base Pole Star was high on the top of a mountain which seemed void of trees but was like pictures of the tundra that Jack had seen in books. A thousand feet below was the tree line and Jack gasped as the immensity of a Norwegian fjord spread out to his view. The fjord was tucked tightly between 2,000-foot-high mountains on either side of the base and could be seen spreading out in the distance as it met the sea. A road below the base had at least a dozen switchbacks as it snaked its way to the water's edge.

Jack took in the magnificent view for a few moments and then went back inside. He quickly showered and dressed and then looked at the clock on the wall. It was only seven a.m.—a little early to see if he could find Annie. He contemplated the last words Dibble had said the night before. Was Dibble actually suggesting that he and Annie go back in time and rescue their adult selves? They were only kids—kids trapped in a nightmare and being asked to do the impossible.

"Atten—hut!"

Jack looked out the window to the parade grounds. The drill sergeant below had called the troops to attention as a distinctive figure came onto the field. It was Com Two, Ethan Dibble. He saluted the sergeant and then turned to the men. Jack could not hear what Dibble was saying but he was impressed with the man's military bearing. He liked Com Two. He liked his passion for the cause of the Coalition. It was completely understandable that he, Jack, would be drawn to such a cause—and drawn to such a friend as Ethan Dibble.

A knock came at the door.

"Come in."

The door opened and a short, stocky young man entered. He wore the Coalition uniform and saluted. "Good morning, sir."

"Good morning," replied Jack, making an attempt to return the salute.

"I'm Cpl. White and I'm here to take you down to breakfast, sir."

"Thanks."

Jack followed the corporal who led him down a ramp at the end of the hallway.

"I trust you slept well, sir."

"I did," replied Jack. "Day starts early around here . . . will you be joining us for breakfast?"

"No, sir. You will be dining with Miss Dibble and her father."

They rounded a corner and came to an open area which was the dining facility. Annie stood by a table in the corner, studying a picture on the wall. She smiled when she saw Jack approach. "Good morning."

"Hi—you okay?"

"Yes, I'm feeling much better."

Cpl. White saluted once again and left the way they had come.

"So, Miss Dibble . . ." Jack looked into Annie's eyes. "What's it feel like? Being dead, I mean?"

Annie glanced away and blushed. "Don't be silly." She looked up. "Here comes my father." Then, she touched Jack's sleeve. "Besides, I seem to recall you followed me to the 'grave.'

"Good morning, Annie, Jack," greeted Com Two as he warmly hugged his daughter. "How did you sleep?"

"Quite well," answered Annie. "Dad, what is it?"

"Oh, it's still so strange seeing you here—I mean, at your age."

"This is a terrible time for you."

"Well, we must do the best we can, mustn't we?" Com Two motioned for the teens to sit as he ordered breakfast.

Shortly, the server brought jugs of milk and juice, eggs on a platter, pancakes, sausages, fried potatoes, and a large bowl of cut-up fruit.

"Talk about a grand slam breakfast." observed Jack. He eagerly dove into the meal and was chugging a glass of chocolate milk when Com Two cleared his throat as if he had an announcement to make.

"Annie, you and Jack are going to have to address the world on the air. And, you're going to have to do it this morning."

"Address the world?" asked Annie. She dabbed her mouth with her napkin.

"*Only* the world," whispered Jack.

49

Dibble smiled. "Yes, the entire world knows you've been killed. That's not good for confidence and morale amongst the Resistance. You need to prove to them that you're still alive over Radio Free America."

"But, Dad, everyone will know I'm not the *real* Annie Dibble—I—I mean, that I'm not the *grown-up* version of myself." Annie looked at Jack. "Is that right?"

"Close enough," he said.

"We've already taken care of that. Over the radio, it won't matter, but we'll be needing some publicity shots one of these days. At sixteen years old, you are close to the same basic skeletal structure of your 36-year-old future self. Interestingly enough, we've determined that you have only gained approximately four pounds in body mass in those twenty years. It still might be necessary to intervene somewhat."

Annie stared at her father in disbelief. "What do you mean by intervene?"

"You're wearing your hair differently these days. And, your clothes—we'll fetch some of Annabelle's and . . . and we'll hire a make-up artist to make you age twenty years. Don't worry, it's state-of-the-art. People specialize in disguises these days. They do a marvelous job, actually."

"Uh, what about me, sir—how much extra weight have I—er, my future self—how much has *he*, that is, have *I* put on—in twenty years, that is?" stumbled Jack.

Annie gave Jack a half smile. "Having trouble articulating?"

"Jack, I just saw you last week when you flew into the base for a council meeting." He grinned. "At thirty-seven years old, you haven't gained a pound unless it's in muscle; in fact, you were up before the troops out running the track the morning you arrived." Dibble scratched his chin. "The trick will be bulking you up from your present condition."

Jack turned to Annie. "I'll see you out on the track," he whispered.

Annie ignored Jack's teasing and turned to her father. "And, just how *do* I wear my hair these days?"

"Annie, it's not important, but what is important is that we have you ready to go by ten hundred hours. We've flown in some experts; in fact, they were due to arrive ten minutes ago."

***

The make-up artist was Eduardo Cassini and his staff. What Eduardo lacked in looks, he made up for in personality. His long Italian nose gave him character, Annie thought, and his enormous brown eyes were so expressive that he hardly needed to talk. But, what Annie loved was his out-going, nurturing quality.

"Oh, eet is she!" exclaimed Eduardo when he first saw Annie. "How I have ad-a-mired you for sooo many years!"

Annie merely smiled, said 'thank-you' and sat in Eduardo's chair. Taped to the mirror was a 2036 picture of Annabelle Dibble from which Eduardo was working. When Annie first saw it, she gasped. She wasn't prepared for the cosmopolitan look the picture showed. She was tall and slender in heels and a long sheath dress of black with a string of pearls gracing her neckline. Annie sat still as Eduardo looked at the picture then back at Annie with a pair of shears in his hand.

When Annie emerged two hours later, gone was her simple cotton blouse and peasant skirt. She walked out of the base salon in a tailored black jacket and pencil skirt. Her strikingly blue shirt was offset by long, pearl earrings.

Eduardo had simply trimmed a few inches from Annie's hair, shaped it, and then pulled it back in a soft bun at the nape of the neck. Tiny curls escaped the bun and framed her face. The make-up job gave her a more mature look but her youthful glow still shone through

Jack took a little longer. Thirty minutes after Annie left the salon, Jack walked into the hallway. He wore a military dark-green sweater with epaulets on the shoulders and khaki cargo pants. Eduardo had trimmed his shaggy hair up and around the ear and neatly shaved his neck to military standards. And, he looked like he had gained ten pounds in muscle through the chest. He looked sheepish as Annie smiled.

"All this bulk—you know, I'm planning to work out so it's the real thing. It'll just take a few weeks . . ."

"You look magnificent," said Annie softly. "Especially the haircut."

"Yours, too," said Jack, suddenly at ease from Annie's compliment.

At that moment, Commander Dibble entered the room. "Say, Eduardo, you did a fantastic job. I would never know they weren't real." He stopped and scratched his head. "Well, you know what I mean."

"You theenk so, Commander?" answered Cassini, beaming with pride.

"They look great and just in time for the broadcast. Just follow me," said Dibble. He led the way out of the room and soon they were entering a new wing of the complex. Double doors opened to what looked to Jack like a very high-tech television studio. Dibble introduced them to the studio manager, Capt. Oberg.

"Nice to meet you. Let's get started," said Oberg.

"But, Dad, I can't give an address to the world. What on earth would I say?" said Annie.

"No need to worry. We have the transcript of a speech you gave about a year ago. I had my staff change a few things, but it's good enough to reassure the public that you are indeed still on the job." Dibble handed Annie a sheet of paper and asked her to review it.

"Do I have to say anything, sir?" asked Jack.

"We decided that won't be necessary. But, I do want you standing beside Annie. Those who can still receive video will see that both of you are alive. The word will get out to the radio audience. I can't overstate how important this is—to show the world that the Resistance is not going away."

"Dad, why do they call it Radio Free America if it's a world broadcast?

"Well, when the United Nations was taken over by the Federation, the controls were tight, no freedom of speech, no television and no radio broadcasting of anything except state-controlled propaganda. There were several technologies available for broadcasting audio and video over the borders into America from other locations. Their attempts to scramble the broadcasts failed." Dibble smiled. "I'll bet that has cost Graff a few sleepless nights—they've never been able to override our communications."

"But, why would they call it Radio Free America if it's also video and it's world-wide?" asked Jack.

"If you'll consult your history books, you'll find they did something similar nearly a hundred years ago during World War II. It was called Radio Free Europe. Old Hitler could close off the borders but he couldn't stop the radio waves that broadcast the message of freedom! Annie, it was your choice—the name I mean. You must have read about the original program somewhere. Anyway, it caught on."

Annie sighed and stepped forward. "I think I'm ready."

Jack took his place beside her. "This shouldn't be too hard."

"Easy for you to say—you're not doing anything except standing there looking buff." Annie gave her paper a little shake and cleared her throat.

"All right," said Oberg. "Let's put this one down, guys."

Annie looked nervously at her father. He gave her a wink and a thumbs-up.

Annie leaned in to the microphone and began.

"Ladies and Gentleman, this is Annabelle Dibble, the voice of Radio Free America! My fellow patriots in America and around the world—It matters not where you call home. It matters not your nationality nor the color of your skin. Deep within the heart of every individual is the cherished love for freedom!

"We have seen what oppression can do. The Federation strangles the cry for liberty and strips inherent initiative from each victim it crushes. Each of us is born with the desire to learn, grow, and produce. In a free world, that desire is nurtured and it flourishes, resulting in a society filled with innovative inventions, thriving enterprises, and overflowing prosperity."

Annie paused and pursed her lips. Her grip on the paper tightened. Then, she resumed, her enthusiasm mounting. "The Federation would kill your drive for excellence! The Federation would kill your drive to create! The Federation would kill your drive to accomplish what is in your heart! It has attempted to trample our God-given freedom. It forces upon us suffocating regulations and martial law makes us cower in fear.

"The Federation has placed a wall of domination before us. Let us unite as we beat our fists against that wall. It must be broken down. History has proven time and again that the spirit of freedom cannot be stopped.

"Patriots! My call to you is this: Rise Up! Throw off the shackles of the Federation and band together. The Coalition is alive and well. Take heart because we are winning. May God bless America and every country that cries for freedom and may He bless the Coalition of Liberty!"

Jack looked at Annie. "That was wonderful."

Beads of perspiration were on her forehead and her eyes were moist. "Thank you." Annie turned to her father. "Did I write this?" she asked.

"Every word."

Annie folded the paper neatly and put it in a side compartment of her handbag. She walked up to her father. "I believe every word I just read. It was marvelous. But, I don't know enough about what's going on in the world, Dad—not like Annie Dibble. I can see by that speech that she knows what to tell the people—I can't fake being her. I can dress like her and fix my hair differently, but I'm not her—at least, not yet."

Ethan Dibble put his arm around his daughter. "We'll figure some things out, Annie. Don't worry. I have an incredible staff that can help with—"

"Dad, it's no good—I'm not her!" Annie dabbed at her eyes with a tissue. "We've got to get Annie back." Annie looked deeply into the eyes of her father. "We've got to get Radio Free America's Annie Dibble back," she repeated quietly.

Nine

The Star of David hung on a tall column in the Ben Gurion Airport and to the left was the warm greeting, 'Welcome to Israel.' Annie followed Jack, Eli, and Capt. Garcia across the lobby of the main terminal.

Jack was wearing jeans and a tee shirt with a baseball cap pulled down over his eyes. Annie's butter-yellow capris matched the band around a floppy sun hat. She nearly lost her dark sunglasses when she looked down to admire her new leather sandals. Lt. Emma Shaw who had been their escort on the first evening at Pole Star had taken her down to one of the local Norwegian towns and they had done some shopping for the trip to Israel. Her skirt and blouse were safely in the closet of her quarters at the Coalition base. The only thing that Annie would not give up was her handbag.

The night before, Com Two gathered Jack and Annie in his office with members of his staff to outline their mission. Jack and Annie would be escorted by Capt. Garcia to Tel Aviv and Eli would go for support. When Jack found that Garcia was going along, he almost opted out.

"He hates my guts," said Jack bluntly. "Commander, I don't blame him one bit, after what happened yesterday. Because of me, a man is dead."

"Because of circumstances beyond your control, a man is dead. There are casualties in war, Jack."

"We can argue this all day; but, like I said, Garcia hates my guts. I don't see how you run an operation with that kind of animosity."

"I've spoken to him about that. He agreed to tone it down—Jack he's my best officer for this kind of thing."

Jack stood shaking his head in frustration. "He acts like he'd kill me if he thought you weren't looking."

"Let me explain something—you don't understand what kind of man Garcia is. He is loyal to a fault, very devoted, and would die for the Coalition cause. He was very dedicated to Com One. They were close associates—you can't imagine how Com One's death has affected him."

"But, I *am* Com One!"

"No you're not—not yet, anyway. And, going against his orders back at FOPS headquarters showed him just that. In his mind, Com One would never have done anything to jeopardize the mission."

"Tell that to Eli."

"Jack, I'm cutting you a lot of slack—I know you have no experience, no training and you did what you felt was right. But, from here on out, Capt. Garcia is your commanding officer. I'm simply not sending you and Annie out there without the best possible protection." He took a deep breath. "Are we understood?"

Jack lifted his head. "Yes, sir."

***

Thirty minutes later, the members of the mission were seated in a semi-circle around Dibble's desk. The first thing Com Two did was show Jack and Annie how the chronometer worked. There were four in all and they lay face up on the desk.

Dibble picked one up and twirled it between his fingers. "First off, this is called a chronometer. You will notice that it is slightly thicker than an old-fashioned pocket watch. It fits nicely in the palm of your hand, but there's a mechanism on the backside that you need to know how to utilize." He turned it over and made sure everyone could see. "There are several display windows and the buttons to regulate them. This one on top shows the date where you are going and this one below shows the location coordinates of where you are. Now, like an ordinary pocket watch, there is a small knob or dial on the very top. Once your time destination is set, you merely push it down and then—"

Jack looked up. "And, then . . ."

"Then, off you go—you are in another time dimension. Mind you, be aware of the time aura when you push the dial. Eli, would you care to enlighten us on the time aura?"

"Certainly, sir. The time aura is the radius around the individual who bears the chronometer. Whoever is within that radius will travel with you to your time destination."

"How big *is* the radius?" asked Annie.

"The aura extends twenty-five centimeters around the individual," answered Eli. He sat perfectly erect in his chair, hands grasping the chair arms, with his feet flat on the floor. Annie wanted to tell him to relax.

"Twenty-five centimeters?" asked Annie.

"A little less than a foot," replied Eli.

"When I was timesnatched, I woke up disoriented and weak," she said.

"That is because you were within the aura. We have discovered that if you are in possession of the chronometer, you will be free of those symptoms."

"That's good to know," said Jack. He glanced quickly at Capt. Garcia who remained stone-faced, his attention turned to the commander.

Dibble continued. "It will be necessary to remove your bohrium bracelets; Capt. Garcia will take care of that detail before you make the time jump. As you know, time travel is not possible if you are wearing them."

"At 0600, you will board the heliplane and arrive at Ben Gurion airport at 0800. From there—"

"Excuse me, sir," said Jack with raised hand.

Com Two said nothing but nodded his head in Jack's direction. Garcia sat back in his chair, his face as hard as stone.

"That's only two hours."

"Correct."

"Two hours to fly from Norway to Israel?"

"Yes, now may we proceed?"

"Yes, sir."

Dibble cleared his throat. "Are there any questions?"

No one spoke. Annie fidgeted with her bracelet, wondering how it was to be removed, and Eli still sat stiffly in the chair.

"All right, then, you will be escorted through the airport by a special envoy who will be briefed as to your mission. Security in Israel is the tightest in the world and you will need to pay strict attention and cooperate on every level. You will eventually be turned over to Coalition agents who will drive you to the café where the unfortunate incident occurred."

Garcia looked visibly agitated. He leaned forward in his chair and put his head in his hands, raking his fingers through his hair.

"Capt. Garcia alone has the details of the time departure, so follow his orders implicitly. It's important to note that it is altogether possible that you may catch a glimpse of the 2036 Jack Flint and Annabelle Dibble after the time exchange. This could happen in the restaurant. Whatever the case, do *not* let it deter your focus on the mission. As soon as you see they have disappeared, exit immediately and rendezvous with the Coalition agents. They will take it from there."

"Excuse me, sir, but is that all there is to the mission? We just walk into a restaurant and then walk back out?" asked Jack.

"Yes, that's all there is to it. It's only important that we deter Com One and Miss Dibble; that is, the future Jack and Annie, from staying in the restaurant. In that way, they will be safely relocated at the time of the explosion."

"Excuse me, sir, but where will they be relocated?" asked Jack.

"As long as you and Annie are on this time level, Com One and Miss Dibble will be relocated to another time continuum—to an alternate time continuum."

Jack knit his eyebrows and said nothing.

"Jack, the best way to comprehend all this is to read Wycliffe's book on time travel. That will have to suffice us for now."

"Yes, sir." Jack shifted in his seat nervously. "One more question, sir—what about all the other people at the restaurant?" asked Jack.

"Jack, I know it seems a simple thing to shout 'fire' and evacuate the facility, but we have been warned strictly to keep time alteration to a bare minimum. We are already stretching it to the maximum. The consequences can be quite grave."

"I'm not going to shout 'fire'."

Garcia lifted his head and glared at Jack.

Com Two laid the chronometer on his desk with the others. He walked over to the windows and stood for a moment. Then, he turned sharply on his heel. "Nicolas Wycliffe has outlined in his book the unfortunate circumstances of his first attempts at time travel. Trust me, Jack. Meddling with time is dangerous at best and foolish at least. In this instance, we have no choice—we *must* rescue Com One and Miss Dibble, so we will proceed. May I have your word that you will follow Capt. Garcia's orders to the letter?"

Garcia's glare continued to bore holes through Jack. The room was silent except for the ticking of the wall clock.

"Yes," said Jack, quietly. "If he's the one giving orders, I'll do as I'm told."

***

An Israeli envoy arrived just beyond the Star of David to escort them, just as Com Two had said. Eduardo had convinced Jack and Annie before they left that a good portion of the world would recognize who they were if they didn't take measures to hide their identities, so Jack had donned the baseball cap and Annie hid behind the floppy sun hat and dark glasses.

They followed the men who were in plain clothes through the terminal and through the VIP area. After a minimum of paperwork, they climbed into a black SUV, left the terminal and began the nine mile trip to Tel Aviv. Annie, wide-eyed, was taking in all the sights through the darkened windows of the SUV. The almost-tropical sunshine was a sharp contrast to the cool Norwegian winds atop the mountain they had left hours before. She was used to living in a city, but Tel Aviv held sights nonexistent in faraway England. Her stomach churned. She knew she was in good hands, but sometimes she just longed to be back at Wigan's Pier, reading Jules Verne. Then, there was the tension between Jack and Garcia. It was tangible, but Garcia's fight was with Jack, and she kept her distance from the man. It was plain that Garcia didn't trust Jack to follow orders; he had kept a sharp eye on the boy from the beginning of the journey. Annie felt Jack had learned his lesson. He had acted on his best intentions in rescuing Eli; after all, Jack was just a kid like her. How could he be expected to act like the commander of a worldwide resistance movement? She hoped that Garcia could understand that fact.

The vehicle wound its way through palm-lined streets where crowds of tourists and shoppers congregated on the street corners. Annie began to feel a little car-sick and leaned back against the seat.

"Feeling okay?" asked Jack.

"Just a bit jittery. I hope Eli is right. I mean, since I have my own chronometer, I shouldn't feel ill when we go back."

"Stay close to me and take my arm if you get dizzy. We're only going to be in the past for a minute and then we'll come right back."

Annie nodded her head and closed her eyes, clutching her handbag. "I'll be all right."

The SUV began creeping a little slower as traffic thickened. They were inching their way down Hertzel Street when the restaurant came into view. There was police caution tape all around the area where the blast had occurred just hours before. Emergency vehicles were parked everywhere and workers were clearing away debris. The driver of the SUV pulled into a side alley and stopped.

Garcia ran through a checklist with everyone on the team. First on the list were the chronometers; each person on the team had been issued one. He asked Eli and Jack if they had their issued handguns. They all answered in the affirmative. "All right, let's see your bracelet, Flint."

Jack put his arm forward. The shiny bohrium bracelet glittered even in the subdued light of the vehicle. Garcia withdrew a small object from his pocket that resembled a small cigarette lighter. He held it over the bracelet and flipped a catch on the contraption which produced a blue beam of light. Instantly, the bracelet fell from Jack's wrist into Garcia's hand. "You won't need this until you get back." With that, he slipped it into a black bag at his feet. Annie and Eli went through the same process, relinquishing their bracelets to the bag.

"Ready?" asked Garcia.

Everyone nodded.

"Okay, the explosion occurred at 1100 hours." Garcia turned to Annie. "That's eleven o'clock a.m. We'll set our chronometers for 1045, fifteen minutes before the incident. Com One and Miss Dibble will already be sitting in the southeast corner of the restaurant. Eli and I will take a seat at the counter near the door. Jack and Annie will enter the establishment. According to time laws, Com One and Miss Dibble should disappear. Jack, you take Annie as soon as that occurs and exit the place. Eli and I will meet you down this alley back by the green fence. We'll get back to the present and mission accomplished. Any questions?"

Jack checked out the location of the green fence Garcia mentioned as he looked through the back window. He felt a surge of excitement race through him. He could feel the small handgun on his belt which gave him a boost in confidence as he exited the vehicle. He helped Annie out and they stood beside the car, waiting for the others.

Annie's nerves were tingling all over and she found herself trembling. The bright blue sky blazed above and the palm trees overhead waved in the gentle August breeze. She looked at Jack and wondered at his ever-present confidence. Nothing seemed to bother him. Even when they first met under the strangest of circumstances, neither having any idea where they were, he kept focused and strong. She watched as the others left the SUV and lined up behind it. She felt as if she were embarking on a roller coaster ride.

Garcia passed out the chronometers to Eli, Jack, and Annie. Annie's hand trembled as she took it. "All right, this is it," said Garcia. "The meters have been set— they're ready to go." He palmed his chronometer. The members of the team watched for his cue. He put his index finger over the button on the top as everyone followed his lead. "Ready, three, two, one . . .now."

Jack pushed the tiny button and felt a surge forward that almost knocked him off his feet. He reached out for Annie and felt her fall gently against him. The world around him was spinning as if it were caught in a giant tornado. Only he and the team seemed to be at a standstill. Then, as quickly as it began, it stopped.

"Everyone okay?" asked Garcia.

"Y—yes," stammered Annie. She looked up at Jack. "Thanks for catching me—I thought I had my balance."

"Flint, you know what to do," ordered Garcia. "Get going."

"Yes, sir,"

Jack took Annie's arm and began leading her toward the restaurant. The rubble and emergency vehicles were gone and there was no yellow caution tape barricading the scene of the terrorist blast. And, the black SUV had disappeared.

"It's so strange—so eerie—that in a few moments this will be a scene of disaster," whispered Annie to Jack.

"I know, and there's nothing we can do about it."

Jack and Annie approached the entrance to the restaurant. "Here we go—keep your eyes peeled for the southeast corner table," said Jack. "We should see Com One and Miss Dibble there, sipping a latte or something, I imagine."

"I imagine," repeated Annie, still trembling.

As they entered through the doorway, loud music greeted them. The place wasn't completely full, but the conversation of the customers was lively. They stood in the entryway a moment scanning for the adult versions of themselves. Jack could see no one that even remotely resembled himself at age thirty-seven and there were at least three tables in the southeast corner that were vacant. There was no one to seat them, so they discreetly moved to the very corner table by the window.

"This isn't working according to plan," whispered Annie.

"I know."

Just then, Garcia and Eli entered the doorway and took seats at the counter. Garcia spied Jack and frowned. Jack raised his eyebrows and shrugged his shoulders.

A waiter approached Jack and Annie's table and they ordered two lemonades. Jack fidgeted as the waiter walked away.

"Eight people are about to die," said Jack under his breath.

"I know. I feel sick about it, but you heard what my father said."

"I'm trying to think what harm could come of saving eight people from being blown to smithereens."

"Jack, let it go."

Jack said nothing.

"There may be dire consequences for changing too much."

"Dire consequences for who? Me? I get squashed out of existence by Garcia for disobeying orders. Meanwhile, eight people get to go home to their families."

"Jack—look," said Annie. She gasped as she stared at the entryway to the restaurant.

A couple had come through the double glass doors of the café. The man was tall and well built; he wore a light summer blazer of blue with a white shirt. He was handsome, clean shaven and his thick black hair was combed straight back. The woman was slim and attractive in a pale yellow summer dress that fell gracefully to her ankles. She looked relaxed and happy, her hand confidently in the crook of the man's arm. It was Com One and Annabelle Dibble of the future.

Jack and Annie glanced at each other. Annie could scarcely breathe as she took in the scene.

The couple walked into the entryway and began looking around for a table. As Com One scanned the room, his eyes drifted toward the two teenagers in the corner. For a moment, young Jack thought the man's gaze fell on him. He wasn't sure and his heart froze. Then, in the time it takes to blink, the man and woman were gone. Jack looked at Garcia who motioned for them to get up and leave. No one in the restaurant seemed to have detected a thing out of place.

"Let's go—we'll get some lemonade back at the base," said Jack. He rose to leave and helped Annie with her chair. Jack looked at the counter and saw that Garcia was already starting for the doorway. Then, in a vision of sheer horror, Jack saw the explosion that would take place in a matter of moments. Men and women were carrying their children through broken furniture and glass and bodies lay strewn around the room. Everyone was screaming and crying and pleading for help. And, then, the vision disappeared and Jack found himself staring down into Annie's face. "Annie, I—"

Just then an Israeli soldier entered the restaurant and yelled, "Everyone exit immediately! Single file—out—*now*!"

The doorway soon became congested with customers. Jack grabbed Annie's hand. "Stay with me," he said as they headed for the back of the restaurant. "Back to the freezers!" he shouted. He ran with Annie beside him behind the counters into the kitchen area, searching for a large walk-in freezer he had seen in the vision. When he found it, he ran to the door and gave a huge pull. The heavy doors gave way and customers and employees began filing in. Then, to his surprise, Eli was by his side.

"You're supposed to be with Garcia!" shouted Jack.

"My direct orders were to see to your safety, Flint."

"Well, let's get in here, then!" Jack shoved Annie into the front corner as several others joined them. When it seemed that no one else was coming, Jack and Eli pulled the doors closed and latched them. Five seconds later, the concussion of the explosion rocked the freezer, shaking the contents of the shelves to the floor. Annie clung to Jack, burying her face in his arm and cried out. Then, all was silent.

Red emergency lights lit the interior of the freezer. Everyone was visibly shaken but no one seemed hurt. Jack grabbed the door handle to open it when a sharp voice shouted.

"You will stay where you are!"

When Jack turned, his heart lurched. Before him stood the skinny figure of the man in the long, blue coat, the man Dibble called Finke, the timesnatcher. He had his arm gripped tightly around Annie's neck and he was arrogantly displaying a gold pocket watch in his hand. "You won't mind if I borrow Miss Dibble for a few moments, will you? General Graff wasn't finished with her." His thumb went up to push the tiny dial to activate the chronometer. At that precise moment, Eli dove at the man, aiming for his hand. But, it was too late. Finke had pushed the dial and Jack stood petrified as he watched Finke, Eli, and Annie disappear into time.

Ten

The left front leg of the charging elephant was lifted, its trunk was raised; and, with a tilt of its head, its tusks were thrust forward like two mighty bayonets. Its red, beady eyes were full of fury and its mouth was open in a silent scream of rage.

Annie Dibble stood before the stuffed beast almost wishing it was alive. At the moment, she would have preferred to take her chances with the elephant rather than face the ire of the man who stood just ten feet away.

"I asked you a question, Miss Dibble."

"And, I believe I gave you my answer." Annie turned away from the enormous elephant that filled half of General Graff's office in the Federation headquarters building in New York City.

"Yes—your impertinent answer!" said General Graff, his lips flapping as he spoke. "You have no idea with whom you are dealing."

"So, you are asking me to recant the things I said over Radio Free America?"

"I am not asking. You will submit to my wishes and you will do it willingly."

"And, just *when* did I give that speech? You keep snatching me out of whatever time I happen to be in." Annie stepped away from the general. "It's quite confusing."

"You gave your speech not four hours ago. I sat in my chair right over there and heard every word. Apparently, our previous conversation had no affect whatever on you."

"Apparently."

"Miss Dibble, you are a very influential force in the world. I intend making you my ally or the world will never hear from you again. I don't plan to set you up as a martyr for your cause, but I can make you disappear. In fact, there are a number of interesting ways to accomplish that. I hope I don't have to show you how it could be done."

"General, when I first came into this warped world of yours, I'll admit I was totally ignorant. I was curious as to what you had to say when Jack and I were first in your office. I've learned a lot since then. If my voice gives hope to an otherwise hopeless world, then I won't silence it—you'll have to do that yourself."

"You will retract every word of today's speech and deliver one I have written myself. Your foolish sentiments will soon be stilled and the world will wonder why they ever listened to your idiotic rhetoric." Graff rang a buzzer on his desk. The side door immediately opened and a young man entered dressed in the Federation uniform.

"Yes, sir," he said as he bowed.

"Smith, you will escort this young woman to the incarceration level immediately."

"Yes, sir." Smith turned sharply and opened the large main doors of the office. At once, two armed guards appeared. They saluted the general in unison.

"We are to escort this young woman to Level 3B," said Smith. One of the guards retrieved handcuffs from his utility belt. He lifted Annie's right arm and pushed back the bohrium bracelet that encircled her wrist and clicked on the handcuffs. Annie's heart sunk more over having the bracelet than the handcuffs. General Graff knew it would make it impossible for anyone to rescue her from another time dimension.

General Graff hovered over Annie as she stood between the two guards. He lifted her chin with his bony finger. "I can assure you that you will be begging to make that speech before this day is over."

Annie jerked her head away and looked at the floor. Her hands began trembling and the dizziness from her time journey threatened to return. She looked at the guards whose faces were expressionless. When was this nightmare going to end? In Tel Aviv, she was looking forward to being back in Wigan by nightfall and now here she was back where she started from. Only this time, she didn't have Jack. Tears welled up in her eyes but she refused to let Graff see them.

***

The guards escorted Annie into the now-familiar hallway and the huge double doors to Graff's office closed behind them. Once in the elevator, one of the guards pushed the 'down' button. Annie bit her lip. How appropriate—down to the lower levels, down to the dungeons. What awaited her there? Were they actually going to torture her into submission?

She thought how similar this was to a book plot she and Gemma made up that summer. The heroine in their book was taken to the dungeons and tortured. Oh, where was Jack with his almost cocky confidence and his unfailing logic? This was no fairy tale and it didn't look like it was going to turn out well.

The elevator stopped at Level 3B where the guards pushed Annie forward into a dark corridor. They opened the second door and turned on the light. The interior was dimly lit. A lone cot with a thin mattress was shoved up in the corner. The guards said nothing to Annie but one touched a button on the wall. "Report to IL 2a immediately. And bring your equipment." He switched the speaker off and motioned Smith and the other guard to follow him out the door.

When the door closed behind them with a hard clank, Annie fell on the cot and buried her face in the flat pillow. Equipment? What kind of equipment? What kind of torture had they devised? She was still sniffling when she lifted her head and looked at her surroundings. There was nothing remarkable about the room—it was painted chalk white and had a low ceiling. A sink was in the corner and she went over to it and splashed water on her face. They had let her keep her handbag and she reached inside for a kerchief. Just then, the door opened and a woman wearing a white lab coat entered. She was blonde and pale with a puffy round face. Her greasy hair was drawn back under a white cap fastened with pins. The woman carried a tray full of what looked like medical instruments. It was then that Annie caught a glimpse of a long, hypodermic needle.

"Sit on the bed," ordered the woman in a thick German accent.

Annie did as she was told. She clung to her bag as if it were a shield but knew nothing would prevent whatever this woman had planned for her. Her insides shuddered and she felt weak.

The woman had her back to Annie. When she turned around, she had the hypodermic needle raised in a vertical position. Her steady hands were covered with blue plastic gloves.

Annie scooted backwards on the cot until her back was up against the cold cement wall. "No!" she screamed, shaking her head. Immediately, the two guards entered the room, shoved her down on the mattress and held her fast. All the while, Annie screamed and tried to break free.

"You will be silent!" growled the woman and she struck Annie across the face. All Annie saw was the blur of the blue plastic medical glove. The next thing she felt was the needle going into the flesh of her right arm. When the guards released her, she fell onto the cot, sobbing. The woman exited the room as quickly as she had entered. The door was shut and the room was completely silent.

Clenching her teeth, Annie examined her arm. There was a tiny red mark where the needle entered, but nothing worse. She rubbed it and wondered if it were a sedative of some kind. She reached into her handbag for a mirror and dabbed at her eyes. Running a brush through her hair, she fastened it back with a ponytail tie. If the shot were a sedative, she would welcome the escape of sleep. She just wanted to obliterate her surroundings. It couldn't come fast enough, she told herself. Then, instinctively, she reached into her pocket where she had put her chronometer from Tel Aviv. The pocket was empty.

Suddenly, the needle mark began tingling and itching. Annie rubbed it gently and then harder. The itching turned into burning. She scratched it until she thought it would bleed—then, the instant she removed her hand, she let out a scream that came from the very core of her being. A black spider was pulling itself up and out of the needle mark. Then, another followed and another until there was a whole line of them crawling up her arm, toward her face, and down her neck. Her hands were a frenzied blur as she swatted at them. They reached her hair and went down her blouse and over her legs. Her eyes were wild with terror as she screamed.

The minutes passed in agony as Annie futilely tried to fling the spiders away. She jumped from the cot and ran to the wash basin. Splashing handfuls of water on the insects, she attempted to flush them down the drain. But, nothing worked. The ugly spiders continued out of her arm and over her body. She ran to the door, banging her fists against it and screaming. "Help, oh help! They're killing me!" Scream after scream emerged until her voice was hoarse and raspy.

Tears streamed down Annie's face and she found herself running back and forth between the wash basin and the door, begging for relief. But, there was only silence. It was useless and Annie felt as though she might faint as she tried to breathe. And, then, as if on cue, the spiders all suddenly dropped from her body and gathered on the floor. In one great mass, they disappeared through the small space under the door.

Annie collapsed onto the cold, cement floor, convulsing in sobs and screams. Her heart was pounding and her breathing was in great gulps. "Help me, please help me!" She closed her eyes and buried her face in her knees. She didn't know how long she sat there clinging to herself, but her heart began to calm and her breathing steadied.

Annie pulled herself up on the cot, trembling. She closed her eyes. What kind of shot had they given her? What else would come out of her arm? Then, a cold blast of air whipped her hair behind her shoulders and snow hit her face. She opened her eyes and, in horror, found herself sitting precariously on a ledge of stone. Snow-capped mountains surrounded her and the ledge hovered over a sheer drop of a thousand feet. The ledge began to tilt toward the abyss. Annie reached for the stone wall she leaned against, her fingernails merely scratching the surface of the granite. Her flimsy, summer shoes gave no traction as she attempted to push herself away from the precipice. "Help! Someone!" But, her screams of terror evaporated into the empty void. She was sliding toward the edge. There was nothing to grab, nothing to cling to and only the vastness of space greeted her as she slipped over the edge into the black expanse. Annie could feel the breath sucked out of her. She felt as though she was screaming with all her power and yet there was nothing but silence. She waited the long seconds for her body to hit the bottom. But, there *was* no bottom— only the sweet smell of long, tall grass. It tickled her nose as she lay in the shade of the largest tree she had ever seen. The air was hot and humid and the sky was a stunning blue through the boughs of the tree. Where was the snow and the black void? What had saved her from certain death? What was the meaning—Annie's thoughts were interrupted by the sound of a thousand trumpets. She jumped to her feet and ran to the edge of the clearing. An enormous cloud of dust was working its way toward her and the ground began to rumble and shake.

Annie's heart began to pound again. What was happening? Should she run? But, she had no time to think—a massive, raging bull elephant was charging toward her, its trunk high in the air and its enormous feet thundering as they met the ground. Its mouth opened and bellowed its raging screams until Annie covered her ears with her hands. Her legs felt like jelly and any effort to run seemed futile. In seconds, the huge beast would be upon her, trampling her to dust. Her own screams were drowned out as the elephant drew nearer and nearer.

Annie had closed her eyes just as the animal reached her and in the blackness all sights and sounds vanished. Her body shook and trembled until she finally lay still.

Moments later, Annie could hear the low vibration and sound of an engine. She was afraid to open her eyes to what she feared would be a new horror. Something was in her hands. It moved back and forth like a wheel. Through squinty eyes, she ventured a look. She was in the cockpit of a small airplane and she was alone. The pilot's wheel was in her hands and the engine was coughing and sputtering. The plane was dipping and diving and straight ahead was a huge snow-capped mountain. With every movement of the wheel, the plane responded. She knew nothing about flying an airplane. The distance to the mountain was growing shorter. She could see the trees along the timber line, tiny lakes glimmering, and massive glaciers just below her. She turned the wheel to the left—the aircraft dipped sharply and Annie screamed once more. She could now see the outcroppings of jagged rocks just a few hundred feet below her. The impact of her tiny airplane was imminent. Its engine sputtered one last time and died. It veered to the right and then to the left. She could see where it was going to crash. The rocks and crags seemed close enough to touch. Annie's hands left the wheel. The image of the mountain was straight ahead. Rocks looked like eyes and a glacier looked like a gaping mouth. With one long last scream, Annie prepared for death. As she raised her arms to shield her face, she felt a vice-grip on her forearms. She tried to shake free. She never knew she had so much fight in her. She struggled against the tightening grip, screaming and trying to twist herself free.

Then, the calmest voice she had ever heard entered into her very heart and soul. "Miss Dibble, Miss Dibble." She opened her eyes. At first, she thought she saw the mountain looming before her, with its rocks and lakes and trees. But, the wheel of the little airplane was gone as was the tilting and diving of the aircraft. Her vision seemed blurred and she couldn't see what had taken the place of the impending doom of the mountainside. The mountain was gone; the lakes were gone; the jagged rocky outcroppings were gone and, in their stead, was the kindly face of Eli.

***

"We have little time." Eli wiped Annie's face with a damp cloth. Her shaking hands told him she was not fully recovered.

"What happened to me, Eli?" asked Annie. She had collapsed into Eli's arms ten minutes earlier. He had gently placed her on the cot, the flat pillow beneath her head.

"They administered a dose of delirimine to you. It must have been small—larger doses have been known to be fatal." He encouraged her to lie still.

"It seems as though I've been gone for days! I've been all over the world, Eli! And, now I'm back in this horrid cell!" Annie buried her face in the pillow.

"It will take some time for you to become re-oriented. You only experienced hallucinations from the drug—it draws upon your greatest fears in an attempt at mind control. One dose is not likely to cause permanent harm."

"Oh, Eli, it was so awful!" Annie covered her face with her hands at the horrible memories. Her hand touched the damp cloth which, by now, had grown warm. She lifted her head, her body still shaking. "H-how did you get here?"

"I was engulfed in the time aura, as were you. Finke took us both into the future and then to FOPS in New York. I have left my cell to help you, but I must return before they discover my absence."

"How did you get out?"

"There is much to explain but this is not the time."

"Take me with you, Eli—please don't leave me—Graff will force me to retract my speech! They tortured me because I refused."

"Miss Dibble, I have a plan, but it will require that we both play our parts well. Yes, General Graff will put you before the cameras. But, if you will trust me, I believe all will be well."

Annie searched Eli's dark eyes. After what she had been through, she felt she wasn't in any position to do anything *but* to trust Eli. "All right—but when will I see you again?" Her grip tightened on his sleeve.

"Very soon. And, here, I want you to keep Timna with you." He gently placed the little creature into the palm of Annie's hand. "She will be a comfort to you until I am able to return." Eli rose and went to the door. But, before he left he turned once again to the girl. "You mustn't be afraid." Eli looked deeply into her eyes. "And, Miss Dibble . . .there are others."

Eleven

Jack stumbled through the rubble of the bombed-out restaurant on Hertzel Street in Tel Aviv. But, it wasn't the overturned tables and broken glass on the floor which caused Jack to stagger and almost fall. It was Annie Dibble's face burned indelibly into his memory; a face filled with horror; a face pleading for rescue. But, he could deliver nothing. He could only stand there, powerless and watch her disappear. In the split second their eyes met, he longed to reach for her and pull her to safety, to pull her away from that monster Finke who now had her in his maniacal grasp. The thought made him physically ill and a great shudder passed through him as his body reeled unsteadily out of the café entrance and into the blazing sunshine.

Jack was just one among many who were emerging from the debris of the bomb, choking on the dust and smoke. He saw the others who had joined him in the freezer standing together across the street. They had escaped unharmed and a measure of relief filled him at least for a brief moment.

Jack ran to the corner of the alley. In the far distance, the sirens of emergency vehicles blared out over the city. Jack knew his best bet was to get out of there as quickly as possible. He remembered Ethan Dibble's warning about time travel as he ran around the corner of the building and saw the green strip of fence at the end of the alley which was the rendezvous point. Garcia was standing there alone.

"Where are Eli and Annie?" barked Garcia as Jack ran up.

"Finke showed up—h-he timesnatched them!" shouted Jack. He thought Garcia was going to punch him and he stepped back. "There was nothing I could do!"

"There's no time to argue about this—we've got to get outa here," shouted Garcia. "Give me your chronometer!"

Jack pulled the instrument from his jeans pocket. Garcia grabbed it out of his hands and flipped the dials on the back. Then, he handed it to Jack. "Ready?" he asked.

Jack nodded and on cue, the man and boy pushed the dials on the top and the world became a twirling time tornado. This time, Jack braced himself; and, when the swirling stopped, he still stood steady on his feet.

The scene at the corner was just as it had been before—yellow caution tape hung everywhere and the same emergency vehicles were as they were before the mission. The black SUV was parked by the side of the restaurant, the driver waiting.

"Hurry—get in the car!" shouted Garcia.

Jack obeyed and slipped into the back seat of the SUV. Garcia jumped in beside Jack and immediately reached for the bag that held the bohrium bracelets. He grabbed one and reached for the instrument with the blue light. He flicked the catch and aimed the blue light at the bracelet. A tiny portion opened up and Garcia slipped it over his wrist. He grabbed Jack's arm and another bracelet and repeated the procedure. Then, swearing, the man threw the bag on the floor and glared at Jack.

"Why didn't you follow my orders?" Garcia's face was red and his breathing was heavy with anger.

"I started for the door with Annie but then—"

Saying nothing, Garcia leaned forward in his seat with both forearms on his knees. Jack thought he was going to flatten him.

"I know this isn't going to make sense, but . . . but I saw the restaurant blow up. And, then I saw the freezer in the back and somehow I knew that was the only chance for Annie and me to make it out."

"Yeah, *you* made it out! If you'd followed my orders, the other two would've made it! It's stupid things like this that put a mission at risk! You're just an idiot kid! I told Com Two I couldn't work with you!"

Garcia opened the back door of the vehicle and got in the front seat by the driver. "Get us outta here!" he shouted.

***

On the two-hour flight from Israel to Coalition Base Pole Star, Jack could think of nothing else but Annie's fate. What time had Finke taken her to? He had made it clear he was taking her to General Graff but even with a chronometer, how could he follow their trail? He closed his eyes in agony as he wondered what Graff had in mind for her. Then, a thought gave him a small glimmer of hope—Eli, too, had been abducted. Eli would do everything in his power to take care of Annie; that is, unless he was eliminated by the Federation.

The heliplane touched down at Pole Star and Jack was shown to his quarters. An hour of pacing in front of the window was finally interrupted by a knock at the door. He was being summoned to Com Two's office.

Escorted on the long walk by Cpl. White, Jack was going over the facts he would present to Com Two. But, how was he adequately going to explain the disappearance of his daughter? Annie had been at least partially under Jack's protection. How could he *not* be blamed for her abduction? And, he would also have to explain the disappearance of Eli. Com Two obviously had a great liking for the young man. Jack took a deep breath as they stood outside the office door. The corporal knocked.

"Come in."

Cpl. White turned the doorknob and entered the office with Jack following. He saluted Com Two as Dibble stood to greet them.

"Corporal, you may be dismissed. Thank you," said Dibble.

After the corporal left, Jack stood humbly at attention. He wished he could crawl under the desk and hide or, better yet, turn and run.

"Jack, please sit down." Dibble motioned toward the chair nearest his desk. "I've ordered some sandwiches in case you haven't eaten."

"Thank you, sir. I—"

"Jack, let's cut to the chase—tell me what happened."

"I—I . . ."

"Capt. Garcia has already given me his version. Now, I'd like to hear yours."

"Sir, there was a glitch right from the start—Com One and Miss Dibble weren't in the restaurant, like they were supposed to be."

Dibble rubbed his chin thoughtfully. "Yes, I remember from the intelligence reports that they had been seated in the far corner table by the window when the explosion occurred. And, they weren't there?"

"Well, no, not at first. I looked at Capt. Garcia for directions, but he was on the other side of the café and so we just waited. And, then, in they came—Com One and Miss Dibble, I mean."

"What did they do?"

"They stood at the entrance for a moment. Com One looked around for a table for just a second and I even thought he saw me, like we made eye contact or something. And, then that was it—they both disappeared into thin air just like Capt. Garcia said they would."

"This was when you disobeyed Capt. Garcia's orders?"

Jack flushed red and stammered. "N-no, sir. I mean, I helped Annie with her chair and we were slowly walking toward the door when ... when..."

"Yes ... what happened?"

"Well, Eli calls it a time signature—I actually saw a vision or something—a premonition of the explosion. I could see the big walk-in freezer at the back of the café and—and I knew we, I mean Annie and I, had to get back there—that it was the only way we were going to survive the explosion."

Com Two continued rubbing his chin. "Go on."

"Just at that moment, a soldier ran into the café and shouted for everyone to get out. Sir, everyone just panicked and headed for the main entrance." Jack raked his fingers through his hair. "So, I grabbed Annie and yelled for everyone to get back to the freezer. A whole group of us ran in. Right then, Eli was standing there and I asked him why he wasn't with Capt. Garcia. He told me his first priority was to protect me. I didn't argue and we just shut the door of the freezer and latched it shut. Seconds later, the bomb went off."

Dibble rose from the chair and sat on the front of the desk. "What then?"

"Eli and I were about to open the freezer when a man told us to stop. When I turned around, that guy Finke had Annie around the neck. He had a chronometer in his hand and said General Graff wasn't through with Annie." Jack stopped and put his face in his hands. "If I could get my hands on that Finke, I'd—"

"Finke is a halfwit. He's one of the Federation goons who go around doing Graff's bidding—nothing terribly complicated, mind you. Timesnatching isn't exactly rocket science, you know."

Jack looked up and frowned. "It is where *I* come from."

Com Two opened the office door when the food orderly knocked. "Over here on the table. Thank you, Corporal." He reached for the cup of tea on the tray. "What else happened?"

"Well, when Eli saw Finke had Annie, he dove for him. He got in the aura and all three of them disappeared. At least by saying Graff wanted Annie, we know where she is—but just not *when* she is." He looked at the food tray but had no appetite for anything.

"Yes, indeed—*when* she is," said Com Two quietly.

"Commander, I'm sorry I messed things up so bad. Capt. Garcia's right—I don't belong on his team." Jack hung his head.

"In some ways, perhaps. But, it was an oversight not to replace the bohrium bracelets precisely when your mission was accomplished. That was not your responsibility."

Jack looked up and stared thoughtfully at Com Two.

"And, there is room for crediting your vision. I know that some people put no credence into time signatures, saying they are a hallucinatory phenomenon. I don't agree—the experiences I've heard lead me to believe there is some validity to them."

"Sir, have you ever time traveled?"

"No, I haven't, Jack. There's never been a need for it. But, that may change now that my Annie is missing."

Dibble took an apple off the tray and returned to his desk chair. "Well, Jack, your story mostly lines up with Capt. Garcia's. Thank you for telling the truth."

"*Mostly,* sir?"

"Yes—he maintains that you disobeyed his orders. And, I do recall that you promised to obey them during the briefing here in my office before your departure."

"But, I *did* obey orders, sir—just not Capt. Garcia's."

"Jack, it complicated the mission," said Dibble, frowning. "If you're going to be a part of our team, you must learn to respect your commanding officer's authority."

Jack sighed. He thought deeply for a moment. "Commander, in the original explosion, ten people died. We rescued two, which left eight people dead. Before I left, I counted eight people filing out of that freezer." He took a deep breath. "And some of them were children."

"Yes, of course," said Dibble.

A firm knock came at the door.

"Come in," said Com Two.

The office door opened and Cpl. White entered, followed by Lt. Shaw and several people in civilian clothes.

"Sir, you'll want to turn on your television right away," said White.

"It's over there, Corporal," replied Com Two, rising from his desk.

Cpl. White clicked the power switch to the television which took up almost the entire wall opposite the windows. Immediately, the face of General Graff filled the huge screen.

". . .the excellent relations with the aboriginal people of the Australian continent. And, now I am pleased to announce a most distinguished guest. It is our privilege at this time to hear the inspiring words of Miss Annabelle Dibble, beloved patriot of the Federation cause. After her stirring remarks, it will be my pleasure to address you. And, now—Miss Dibble."

The camera panned the room and rested at a podium. Standing behind it was Annie. She was still wearing the yellow capris and white shirt Jack had last seen her in. Her handbag was hanging from her right shoulder and her hair was pulled back away from her face. It looked like a sorry attempt by the Federation to make Annie look older. Gone was the sparkle in her eyes and in its place was a look of grim resignation. Jack left his chair and stood a few feet from the screen.

"Are you recording this, White?" asked Com Two.

"Yes, sir."

Dibble inched closer to the television, his mouth a thin line and his fists clenched.

"My fellow patriots . . .," began Annie in a monotone and clearly reading from a script. "It is my pleasure to speak to you today of the unfathomable generosity of the Federation of Peace and Solidarity and of the bounteous charity of our esteemed leader, General Horatio Graff.

"The wondrous accomplishments of the Federation in the past few decades have been marvels of technology. Never in the history of mankind has there been so much cooperation among the peoples of the civilized world. Disease has been eradicated. Poverty has been eliminated. All share in the common knowledge that never again will there be homelessness. Never again will there be joblessness. And, never again will there be confusion as to our purpose on this planet. That purpose is lofty, indeed—we are here to work for the good of all. *Commune Bonum*—for the common good. When we sacrifice our all for the commonality of man, we find our greatest fulfillment. Selfishness and greed have no place in our modern world. Many have been persuaded through our re-education processes to see the benefit of that sentiment.

"So, patriots—let us go forth with renewed energy in support of the Federation and its efforts to civilize the world. If there are those among you who do not share with you a clear vision of the future, recommend them to IRE. Dissenting dialogue will only erode the progress that has been so painstakingly accomplished. No true patriot would want this in their town or city. Speak up and speak to a representative to eliminate any dissent you may encounter. And, now I commend General Graff for his benevolent achievements and present him to you at this time."

"Freeze the picture," ordered Com Two.

With a click of a button on the remote control, Cpl. White obeyed.

A close-up of Annie Dibble filled the huge screen on the wall. No one spoke but all sat in silence as the words of the speech sank in. No one who heard those words believed them to come from Annie's heart. Jack moved closer to the screen and looked deeply into the girl's eyes. They were sad. She looked ashen and weak, as though she were hiding an inner fear. His eyes lifted to her hair. It was combed back in a cold, military fashion. Gone were the soft curls that usually framed her face.

Jack was about to turn away when something caught his eye. He stepped closer to the screen and examined the top of Annie's handbag. The long strap hung from her shoulder and where the strap was sewn into the bag itself was something Jack had not noticed at first.

"Commander, would you come here a minute?" Jack looked in Com Two's direction. "Take a look at Annie's bag—that thing attached to the strap."

Several others moved in for a closer look.

"Yes, I see it." Dibble peered closer. "What is it?"

Everyone examined the object and then looked at Jack.

"Well, if you ask me, it's a little fur ball called Timna." Jack turned from the screen.

"Timna?" Dibble's nose practically touched the screen as he examined the object closer. "Yes, I think I would agree with you."

"That means that Eli's there—he's helping Annie."

"She and Eli *knew* we'd be watching the broadcast so they gave us a clue. At least we know that's she's not alone." Dibble sank down in his chair, visibly relieved.

"I wish there was more," said Jack.

"There *is* more." It was Lt. Shaw. "The Federation building can never hold Eli."

"What?" asked Jack.

"There is certain classified information about Eli, Mr. Flint, which I am not permitted to share."

The room went silent.

"Lt. Shaw is right. Eli won't stay put in a cell at the Fed building. He'll get out and head straight for the city," said Com Two.

Lt. Shaw sighed deeply. "Escape into New York City?"

"Yes," answered Com Two.

"Sir—that, I'm afraid, would be suicide."

Twelve

The right side of Annie Dibble's face still stung from General Graff's forceful slap. Apparently, he did not like her speech. Her upper right arm also ached where his bony fingers had dug into her flesh. He had pulled her away from the podium after her speech and flung her at a waiting guard.

"I expected more," Graff said evenly. His red face was mere inches from hers and his foul breath made her feel queasy. When she recoiled, he slapped her again and had ordered the guard to return her to the prison cell.

Annie now sat on the edge of her prison cot and examined the arm that received the delirimine injection. The point where the needle entered was swollen and red around the edges. And, it itched unbearably. She went to the wash basin and doused it with cool water. It helped for about a minute and then the incessant burning began again.

Annie turned away from the basin and saw her oversized handbag stashed in the far corner of the room. She retrieved it and sat again on the cot, pulling the bag onto her lap. She dug to the bottom of the bag and pulled out a clear cosmetic case. It contained a small tube of ointment and she lavishly applied it to the redness which had now grown to about an inch in diameter. Why was this tiny needle hole becoming so bothersome, she wondered. She had had shots before in her life and never had a reaction. But, then, she had never had a shot of a hallucinatory drug before, either. She hoped that the salve would ease the pain; but, if anything, it had made it worse.

Annie rested her head on the pillow and closed her eyes. If only she were back with her father at Coalition base. There would be doctors there that would know what to do. Then, she sighed. There would also be Jack. He had surely made it back through time with Garcia and they were probably even now planning her rescue. She at least had to hope they were. She imagined the shock Jack must have felt when she and Eli were abducted. How helpless he must have felt.

She looked around the bleak room. At least the last time she had been timesnatched, she had been with Jack. He had kept a cool attitude and didn't panic but sized up the situation as best he could. Even though he wasn't much older than she, Annie felt he was someone she could trust. She knew that the last time she looked into his eyes. They were changeable eyes, sometimes steel-gray like when she first met him. Then, when he was angry at Garcia, they almost seemed black. But, here she was alone, on her own. Except for Eli. Yes, there was Eli. And, what was his visit all about? Had she dreamt it? Was it part of the hallucination?

Annie reached for her handbag and dug into its depths, searching for a piece of paper. Tucked into a corner she felt what she was looking for and withdrew the speech she had given from Coalition Base Pole Star. She unfolded the paper and read the lines which her father had told her she had written herself.

"Ladies and Gentleman, this is Annie Dibble, the voice of Radio Free America! My fellow patriots in America and around the world— It matters not where you call home. It matters not your nationality nor the color of your skin. Deep within the heart of every individual is the cherished love for freedom!

Annie sniffled and folded the speech. The words echoed in her mind, *Take heart because we are winning!*

"Take heart," Annie said softly to herself. Yes, she would take heart. She would bravely face whatever stood in her way. She would take heart and make it through this day.

Annie jerked with a start. Her bag began to vibrate deep down inside. It was crumpled next to her and she almost threw it on the floor when she decided to pull open the top of the bag and peer inside. Two little eyes peered back.

"Timna!" exclaimed Annie. "I almost forgot you were here. It seemed you were part of the hallucinations I had." She pulled Timna out into the light and held her in her hand. "I'm sorry if you got squished in there. You must have jumped in for safety when you saw that nasty old general coming."

She gently stroked the top of Timna's tiny head. The little creature's legs, ears, and tail popped out and she stretched luxuriously. The animal had a remarkable calming effect on Annie. She could feel her whole being begin to relax. If nothing else, it felt good to not be completely alone.

Then, the click of the door latch almost caused Annie to fall off the cot. Her heart pounded wildly in her chest. Could it be the guards with another shot? She knew General Graff was furious with her for her poor delivery of his speech. There was no doubt he would resort to more torture to get her cooperation. Dread filled her soul as she contemplated going through the terrifying hallucinations again. She quickly stuffed Timna back into her bag and rose from the cot.

Annie trembled as she watched the door slowly sliding open. Then, suddenly, Eli was standing in the room and pulled three other people through the doorway.

"Hurry. Close it quietly," whispered Eli.

A boy of about fourteen closed the door, but at the very last moment, the door creaked on its hinges. The boy looked at Eli. "Sorry."

"Eli! How on earth did you break out and get here?" Annie felt like hugging him. Instead, she reached in her bag and showed him Timna. "Look—she's safe and sound. She jumped into my bag after the speech. I had forgotten she was here."

"Indeed, I told her to stay with you while you gave your speech. Perhaps Com Two will see her on the television and know that I am with you."

"That was brilliant, Eli."

"Do you mind keeping her for me—it seems they have confiscated her little satchel."

"Not at all." Annie gently replaced Timna into her handbag. It seemed the little creature had found a comfortable place to sleep in the warm darkness. Then, Annie looked at the three young people Eli had with him. She immediately recognized Lizzy, her friend Gemma's sister.

The last time Annie saw Lizzy, she was wearing a flowing gown to perform for General Graff. She now wore a white shirt with denim pants. Her long, dark hair was in two braids pulled back with a tie. Annie approached her and gave her a hug. "Lizzy, it's so good to see that you're safe. Your family has been looking all over for you."

"Oh, Annie, how did you get here? Did that horrible man kidnap you, too?"

"Yes."

"Why are they doing this to us?" asked Lizzy. Tears formed in her eyes and she wiped them with the hem of her shirt.

But, it was Eli who answered the question. "The individuals who have been timesnatched have proven themselves obstacles to the Federation once they have reached adulthood. General Graff devised a plan to abduct these persons and turn them to his own purposes."

"And, if they won't turn . . ," ventured Annie.

"We really must be moving on. Later, I will answer your questions in greater detail, Miss Dibble. But, for now, we must escape this building. Let me introduce you to Cory Pratt and Preston Jones."

Cory was the one who had closed the door. He had a strong, stocky build—the kind that would interest a football coach and his dark hair was a crew cut in need of a trim. When he grinned, his braces flashed in the stark overhead light.

The other boy, Preston, glanced at Annie and blushed. That only caused his already ruddy cheeks to redden even further. He looked about fifteen and would hardly make eye contact. His blonde hair was shaggy around his ears and ran over his collar. Both boys wore the same clothing as Eli—a simple prison uniform of blue pants and shirt.

"Miss Dibble, I have already briefed the others on our escape plan. Now listen—we will enter the hallway and proceed to the stairwell. We are presently on the third level incarceration area, so we only have three floors to ascend. We will enter the main floor where the lobby is located and the main doors." Eli was focused and calm.

"The main floor? Isn't there a back way?" asked Annie.

"When they detect our absence, the main door will be the least suspected escape route."

Annie nodded.

"I have already disabled the security cameras in the hallway just outside this door. That will give us a clear way to the stairs. Are there any questions?" Eli glanced at each of the four.

"But, how did you get out?" asked Annie.

"There is no time to explain. Now, you will all please follow me." Eli turned to Lizzy. "Stay as close to me as you can."

Annie saw a tenderness in Eli's expression that she had never seen before as he searched Lizzy's eyes. The young man approached the door and quietly pulled it open. He shot a glance in both directions and then motioned for the others to follow.

Annie shouldered her floppy handbag. She was glad to leave the confinement of the cell even though there was no way of knowing what lay ahead for them. Eli's confidence had a calming effect over the entire group as they inched their way down the hallway. It was unheated and dimly lit and had a musty basement smell. They all ducked into the alcove which was the entrance to the stairwell and Eli swung the door to the stairs open wide as the others went through single file. Once on the stairs, the group quickly and quietly climbed to each successive landing. The stairwell was poorly lit and a cold draft came from somewhere down below. They were approaching the third floor from the bottom level when loud voices echoed in the stairwell. Eli motioned for them to freeze.

"Call the command post to sound the alarm!" The man's voice was as clear as if he were standing on the next landing below.

Annie's heart pounded. How were they ever going to get past a heavily-guarded fortress like Federation headquarters? They were just a bunch of children with the exception of Eli. And, he didn't have any kind of weapon that she could detect. At that moment, their attempt to escape seemed completely futile. And, then Annie saw Eli turn to face the wall. His movements seemed mechanical, almost robot-like. He raised his right hand, spread his fingers wide and flattened his hand against the wall. Immediately, a soft, golden light emanated from the space between the wall and his hand. He left it there for no more than five seconds when the glow disappeared.

"Come. It is now safe to proceed," said Eli. He led the way up the last flight of stairs and stopped as they reached the level of the main lobby. "You will all wait here," he ordered. Eli opened the door and slipped quietly through, leaving the other four alone.

More than a minute passed. It was hard for Annie to keep her breathing steady. Cory paced back and forth and Preston was wringing his hands. The wait was becoming unbearable when Eli returned.

"The guards barring our way to the main entrance have left. The foyer is very large—we will skirt around to the right past the doorway. The room is not well lit. Stay within the shadows as much as possible."

"What about the force field in the entrance? We can't get through that." asked Cory.

"Yes, but leave that to me. Is everyone ready?" Eli waited until everyone had nodded in agreement. "Let us exit single file, remaining as close together as possible. Keep your eyes alert." He motioned for them to follow as he swung the heavy metal door open.

The confines of the stairwell contrasted sharply to the enormous lobby of the once-United Nations building. A large, golden ball hung on a pendulum from the incredibly high ceiling and the walls were decorated with elaborate paintings. The group silently crept around the information booth in the middle of the room. Annie looked up and saw the angular-shaped tiers of several balconies above her. She walked closely behind Cory with Preston bringing up the rear. They tried to walk silently on the exotic marble flooring but could not completely muffle their footsteps. Eli was leading them over and around the inside curve of the wall and, in minutes, they were within twenty feet of the main entrance. Annie marveled that there were no actual doors, just a large open space which reminded her of the doorway in the silver cell she once shared with Jack. She also remembered the bloody gash Jack had received for trying to escape.

Eli put his hand up to halt the group. Distant voices were coming from somewhere behind them in the direction of the stairwell they had just left. Eli motioned for them to move behind a tall, slim glass partition, an enormous room divider with a painting hung on it. Annie wished fervently that it was made of steel.

The voices grew louder. Annie trembled at the sound—she knew it had to be soldiers searching for the escaped prisoners. All eyes were turned in the direction from which they had just come. Suddenly, the stairwell door flew open and four armed Federation soldiers burst into the lobby. Their sleek, black weapons were at the ready to fire at the first provocation.

"Why hasn't someone activated the alarm?"

"Sir, I did—they say it's malfunctioning."

"Well, tell 'em to try again!"

The soldiers began a systematic sweep of the room, looking behind every corner and under every piece of furniture. Annie bit her lip. It was just a matter of minutes before they were discovered. She turned to look at Eli. As always, his face was impossible to read. What kind of plan was this? Here they were—sitting ducks for the Federation soldiers to easily find. Flattened up against the wall in the shadows was only going to work for so long.

As the moments ticked away, the soldiers came closer and now were between the information desk and the only thing that separated them—the clear glass wall. Annie longed for the painting that hung on it to be bigger so it could have concealed them. She held her breath in fright until her lungs ached. She was sure that in only a few seconds the soldiers would see them there, clinging to the darkness.

Then, to Annie's right, Eli took a step toward the glass partition. The shadows still concealed his presence as he placed his hand flat against the smooth glass surface of the divider. Instantly, the soft, golden glow appeared again between Eli's hand and the glass. And just as instantly, one of the Federation soldiers opened fire.

"Run through the door—I have disabled it!" shouted Eli, his hand still glowing on the partition. "Annie! Take them and run—I will follow!" The commanding voice of Eli was so compelling that Annie immediately obeyed. She grabbed Lizzy's arm and dragged her out of the shadows.

"Boys! Follow me!" shouted Annie. She dashed through the door, pulling Lizzy behind her.

As Eli stood with his hand outstretched on the glass, a rain of bullets ricocheted off the partition. More gunfire followed, but the shimmering glass remained unharmed, protecting Eli and the four children. Eli watched as Preston, the last of the four, slipped through the main doors and disappeared. With a sudden jerk, Eli removed his hand from the glass divider and ran in the direction of the doorway. No sooner had he pulled his hand away than the entire wall collapsed in a mountain of broken glass crystals. By now, Eli had reached the outside of the doorway and yelled at Annie and the others to keep running.

The soldiers in the lobby stopped their shooting. Eli knew the enormous pile of broken glass would slow them down but it would be only moments before they stormed through the main entryway. Eli touched the outside of the doorframe and ran. He had not run ten feet when behind him he could hear the cursing of the men and the clacking of weapons hitting the marble tile floor. A quick glance behind him confirmed that all four soldiers had run into the invisible force field that had been meant for Eli and his friends.

A surge of energy filled Eli and he ran around the corner of the building—he could faintly see the shadowy outlines of his companions in the darkness ahead. Just then, several Federation guards opened fire. Eli sprinted at lightning speed past the outer perimeter of the Federation grounds. In seconds, he was beside the time children running with all his energy, grasping Lizzy's hand, and pulling her alongside him.

"Run! Run for all you are worth!" shouted Eli.

With every bit of energy they possessed, the children ran. Annie's sides ached and her arm was on fire but she ran. They were getting away—away from the bullets of the soldiers; away from the evil of General Graff and into freedom, into the unknown and into the blackest night Annie had ever seen.

Thirteen

The booming voice of Capt. Garcia, like an approaching locomotive, started faintly behind Jack and then grew louder with its heavy rhythm beating a military cadence. Soon, the captain was running next to Jack as the young man ran in step with the chant.

"Left—right. Left—right. C'mon, Flint, if you can't keep up, you'll find yourself back at base mopping floors! Now, move it!"

Jack's pulse rose as he seethed with anger. He was far from the last man in the military formation of soldiers. They were running on a treacherous mountain trail a half mile above Coalition Base Pole Star. Garcia had hounded him practically every mile of the run.

The night before when Com Two indicated Jack would be accompanying them on Annie's rescue mission, Garcia sharply objected. "Commander, isn't it obvious by now that this kid is nothing but trouble? There have been two missions and two mess-ups because of him."

"I understand your concerns, Captain," Dibble had said. "But, with your proper supervision and training, I have high expectations that some of these shortcomings can be remedied."

Garcia left Com Two's office in icy obedience. If Jack was to go on the rescue mission and Com Two wanted Jack trained, then trained he would be—to Garcia's standards. Jack soon realized it was Garcia's path to revenge and an attempt to weed him out of the mission.

Garcia had ousted Jack out of bed at 5:00 that morning and drilled him ruthlessly right from daybreak. Jack held on, determined to win at Garcia's game. Besides, Jack was not in poor shape; after all, he was scheduled to play linebacker in the 2016 football season for Teton High. In fact, they were scheduled to begin practice next week. Jack shook his head. Next week—when was that? Twenty years ago? Or twenty hours ago? Would he be forever in this time trap of impossible trips into the future, where pocket watches were time machines and silver bracelets were not jewelry?

So, here he was, three thousand feet above an azure-blue fjord in Norway, running along a trail sometimes barely wide enough to accommodate his running shoes. The trail followed the tops of the mountains that hid the base from the outside world. The tundra-like area was above timberline and one misstep would plunge a runner headlong down the hill to the heavy pine forest below.

"C'mon, keep up! One—two! One—two! Garcia's voice carried back to Jack from somewhere far ahead. Half a mile later, the captain finally showed some mercy to the squad. "Okay. Knock off. Ten minutes!"

Jack and the other runners breathed heavily and brushed the sweat off their brows. No one had carried any canteens of water or backpacks. Jack was looking around for a stream to drink from when a mechanical whirring noise came from behind him. He turned in time to see a large boulder open up to reveal a large refrigerated unit full to the brim with bottles of cold drinking water. No one but Jack seemed the least surprised by the machine and a line soon formed for the water bottles. After grabbing one, Jack picked a rock to sit on to down his drink.

"This altitude can be a killer," said a voice next to him. Jack glanced over and saw that it was Cpl. White.

"Yeah, this is quite a run, but where I come from, the altitude is twice what it is here. That is, if that's the ocean in the distance. I would guess we're at about three thousand; my home is at six." Jack sipped his water as he gazed into the distance where the fjord met the sparkling sea. Two white ocean liners were making their way up the inland waterway. His eyes lifted from the level of the ocean up through the timber of the mountains and then to the relatively bare tundra on which they had been running. "Never seen country like this. From ocean to mountaintop just like that." He snapped his fingers for emphasis.

White nodded as he caught his breath. "Yeah—it's really something. Hey, we'll be doing rifle practice this afternoon—you'll get to work with the AKS. They're kinda like the old AK-47 of your day."

"That remains to be seen," said Jack.

"What do you mean?" asked White.

"I'll be practicing rifles only if Garcia says so." Jack stood up.

"Hey, it's time to go," said White as he threw his empty bottle into a large trash bag. "Back to the trail, Com One—I mean, Flint," stuttered the corporal. As White left, Capt. Garcia immediately appeared from around a rock.

"There may be some who think you're Com One, but you're a far cry from it," snarled Garcia.

Jack remained silent.

"In fact, comin' on this rescue mission is a big mistake. You're no soldier—you can't follow orders and you have a habit of takin' things into your own hands. You're a liability I can do without."

"I never volunteered for it," stated Jack.

"Then, tell Com Two you're droppin' out."

"He wants me along."

"Well, all I can say is you better not mess up this time. You've done that twice." Garcia started off down the trail.

"Well, third time's the charm," added Jack. He wasn't sure if Garcia heard him. The man was already twenty feet ahead of him.

Later that afternoon, the drill instructor placed an AKS in Jack's hands. He hefted the sleek, black weapon, admiring its unique engineering. Years of hunting and target practice had honed his skill as a marksman. This clearly irritated Garcia. Jack's target was nearly perfect, but a fact Garcia ignored. Jack was sure the captain hoped incompetence with the gun would have disqualified Jack from the mission.

Finally, the day ended after hours of briefings by Garcia on military strategies and historical war dramas. At almost eleven p.m., the captain allowed him to go. Jack, exhausted, dragged himself to his room and fell asleep as soon as his head hit the pillow.

***

Ethan Dibble's metal-rimmed spectacles were slowly sliding down his nose. He made a mental note to have them adjusted just as soon as he was through reading his latest book. His back ached from having his feet propped up on his desk when suddenly his stomach growled. He sighed and looked at the clock. It read '0200.' He was not usually in the habit of staying up half the night reading, but the information for which he was searching was vital. He marked his place and set the book face up on his desk. It's shiny red and black cover read, *"The Intricacies of Time Travel."* Inscribed on the lower edge were bold letters which spelled out the author's name, Nicolas Wycliffe.

"We must keep our wits about us," mumbled Dibble to himself. "Too much could go wrong."

A knock came at Com Two's door. Dibble swung his feet to the floor and was coming around the edge of his desk when the door opened a crack.

"Sir, Commander . . . I saw your light on—may I have permission to enter?" It was Jack Flint.

"Yes, my boy. What on earth are you doing up at this unholy hour?"

"I can't sleep anymore—I think all the training today got me wired."

"Capt. Garcia has been quite the taskmaster, I hear."

"Um . . . no, sir. I mean . . .it's been good for me," stammered Jack.

"Yes, I daresay the chap can be a bit hard-nosed; but, then, he's usually my top choice for any mission requiring a level head and good instincts. You may thank him someday."

Jack nodded but said nothing.

Com Two returned to his chair.

"Sir, I can't think of anything but Annie—I mean, to think of her in the clutches of that dim wit Finke. Commander, what are our plans to rescue her?"

"Believe me, Jack, I'm working on it every minute. There are some particulars to time travel that we must be absolutely clear about. I'm studying Wycliffe's book." Dibble removed his glasses and used them to point to the book. "Help yourself while I go downstairs for a bite to eat. Would you like me to get you anything?"

"No, sir—I'm not hungry." Jack retrieved the book from Dibble's desk and settled into a sofa near the huge television screen where he had seen Annie's image just the day before.

"I'll return soon—see what you can learn." With that, Com Two left Jack in the silent and softly-lit office.

Jack read the title of the volume and then flipped to the back of the jacket where there were several endorsements:

"Impossible to put down if you have any interest in time travel. The only logical conclusion I could come up with was you better have a dang-good reason for doing it." –Will O'Reilly

"Mr. Wycliffe has assembled an incredible digest of data of the caliber usually encountered in the loftiest scientific libraries of the world."—The London Times

"After reading the amazing account of Wycliffe's attempt to rescue his grandfather, I looked at the subject with a totally new attitude—complete respect for the author and gratitude that I don't have a chronometer!"—Dr. Everett Brown

Jack looked at the inside back flap and stopped. There was a full-color photograph of the author and a short biography. The man was sitting in a leather chair with his arms across his knees, a pipe in one hand. He looked like the grown-up version of the *Wonder Kids* hero at the drugstore comic book stand. Shaggy lashes fringed his brilliant blue eyes which were magnified by thick, dark-rimmed eyeglasses. An unruly cow-lick forced his brown hair straight up in the front and over to the side. Jack read with interest the short biography below the picture:

Nicolas Wycliffe, renowned physicist and inventor, is the author of three London Times bestsellers: 'My Race Through Time', 'Quantum Triumphs', and 'The Year I Never Existed.' A native of Danby, England, he graduated from Oxford University with a degree in quantum physics. Dr. Wycliffe has served in many supervisory capacities at the University and currently is conducting research at the Nanoscale Physics Research Laboratory. Wycliffe lives near Danby with his wife and two small children.

Jack turned the book over and flipped through the pages, stopping frequently to read. Most of the book was over his head until he came to a page with the heading *Time Levels*. He skipped to the third paragraph.

"The present time in which one exists is to be considered Time Level One." Jack read aloud softly. *"Transporting to the future or past will constitute Time Level Two. If one is predisposed to go forward or backward yet again, the result would be that the individual is experiencing Time Level Three and so on and so forth. Extreme caution must be exercised when manipulating time levels. We lose the linear motion of the time continuum as we add time level to time level. This I experienced acutely during my horrific journey to my grandfather's century."*

Jack set the book down and took a deep breath. According to Wycliffe, Jack was in time level two. He had been in time level two until he was transported into the future in Tel Aviv. Then, he had been in level three. But, when he and Garcia had gone back in time after the explosion, he returned to level two.

Jack jumped off the sofa, nervously raking his fingers through his hair. "This is bad—this is really bad. Annie is —" Just then, Com Two came in the door with a tray of food in his hands.

"Commander! Sir, I just read something in that book that's really disturbing! It's about time levels and they're numbered according to how many times you go—"

"Jack, sit down and have a cup of tea."

"But, sir—Annie is in time level *four*! Wycliffe says that's really bad. We've got to get her out of there!"

Ethan Dibble sat the tray on his desk, reached for a steaming cup and sank into his chair. His eyebrows knit into a frown and he bit his lip. "Yes, I read that part recently and it has me gravely concerned. You see, Wycliffe discovered that the higher the time level you experience, the more difficult it is for chronometers at lower levels to locate you."

"Chronometers can locate people in different time levels?" Jack sat in the chair next to Dibble and leaned forward.

"Yes. The individual who has time traveled leaves what is known as a time trail. A chronometer on the time level just below or above the individual can actually trace that individual using the person's time trail. I am tremendously worried that Annie's time trail may be undetectable." Dibble sipped his tea and then set the cup on the end table. He lifted his eyes and stared into space.

"But, we know where she and Eli are—they're in New York City. Can't we just go there? Won't we be able to find them at Federation headquarters?"

"It's not that easy, Jack. It's imperative that we find Annie at the time level to which she was taken. Yes, we could probably find her and Eli at the Fed, but they wouldn't be *the* Annie and Eli that we need. I know it sounds mad, but the complications of time travel are not to be trifled with. 'Twisting the threads of time' is what Wycliffe calls it. And, he says it's nearly impossible to untwist them."

Just then, the telephone on Com Two's desk rang. Dibble picked up the receiver. "This is Com Two. Yes, I'm up. Of course, Lt. Shaw, come up immediately." When he hung up the phone, he looked at Jack. "Lt. Shaw says there's something important that's come to her attention."

***

Jack knew very little about chronometers. So, when he saw the dials spinning on the one Lt. Shaw held in her hand, he just blinked and stared blankly at the little gold machine.

"What do you make of this, Commander?" asked Shaw.

"I don't know," he answered. "Get Garcia up here."

Five minutes later, Capt. Garcia strode into the office where Com Two, Lt. Shaw, and Jack Flint sat around the chronometer captivated by its strange behavior.

"Captain, get over here and look at this," said Com Two. "I've never seen anything like it—maybe you have an idea."

Garcia took the chronometer in his hand and watched the dial spin in a blur. "The location coordinates are supposed to turn when seeking a time trail, but I've never seen one spin like this. I don't know—chronomium has properties we're still discovering. Or, so I've been told, sir."

"Lt. Shaw, is this the only one that's behaving in this manner?" asked Dibble.

"No, sir. All the ones we used in Tel Aviv are doing the same thing."

Dibble held his chin, scratching as he paced back and forth in front of the massive television screen. The room fell into silence as everyone considered what the spinning dials could mean." Jack glanced at the clock on the wall. It was 0300 hours.

"Sir, look at this," said Lt. Shaw. She held the chronometer out for Commander Dibble to see.

Com Two picked up the time machine and examined it. All the dials on the backside had come to a complete stop. "Captain, what do you think?" he said.

"I don't know, but can I check something?" asked Garcia.

"Of course."

Garcia, with the chronometer in hand, slid into Com Two's desk chair and began typing on the computer keyboard. Drumming his fingers on the desk, he waited for something to come up on the screen. When it did, he let out a shrill whistle.

"What is it, Garcia?" asked Com Two.

"In the coordinates dial on the chronometer, sir. You know, the one that gives the location coordinates—it's giving an exact location. My guess is that it's Annie's location. Someone on her end is sending this stuff."

Dibble walked to the computer screen and read what Garcia had called up. "Where, Garcia? Where is it pointing to?" His voice was shaking.

"New York City, sir—right in the heart of Manhattan."

Fourteen

When Eli hurled himself around the corner of the Federation building, he had run past two guards who stood beyond the main entrance. Instantly, they had opened fire on the sprinting escapee. Their bullets rang out into the night but made no connection with their target.

"That's impossible—we couldn't *both* have missed!" shouted one of the guards.

"Must be losin' my touch," said the other. "Doesn't matter—get back to your post—they won't survive an hour out there."

Eli's lungs heaved as he sprinted toward four shadowy figures. "Run!" he shouted as he grabbed Lizzy by the hand. He took a sharp turn toward the river as the others followed. The brilliantly-lit Federation building was slipping behind them, and the East river was a barrier to the front. In seconds, they reached a barricade and ran alongside the waterway toward the skyscrapers which could be seen dimly in the faint starlight.

"It's so dark," gasped Annie. "This can't be New York City—has there been a power outage?"

"Keep running!" shouted Eli.

The band of escapees ran along the waterfront until they could run no more. Annie was the first to stumble and fall. She collapsed in a heap on a grassy area.

"Go on without me!" Annie was gulping air and coughing. "Oh, please—my arm is on fire!" She grabbed her arm and held it to her chest.

"Miss Dibble—we must get farther away from the Federation building. Please, I can help you." Eli lifted her to her feet with ease and pulled her along. Annie's lungs ached and she longed to collapse again and rest.

The obscure outlines of skyscrapers loomed all around as the group plunged deeper into the depths of the city. The warm August air was heavy with humidity and the stench of rotting garbage was like a tangible barrier.

"What's that stink?" asked Cory. "It smells like a dead body."

"We must keep moving," replied Eli. He led them through the deserted streets. On every side were piles of rubbish and burned-out cars. Store fronts were smashed in and broken glass glittered on the pavement of the sidewalk. Dogs roamed the streets and snooped in overturned trash cans. Annie began whimpering.

"I'm sorry, Eli. It's more than I can bear." The tears streaming down her face glistened in the faint light. She took another step and then fainted.

Eli knelt by Annie's side and with one swooping motion, picked her up as if she weighed no more than a small child. "We must find shelter," he whispered. He glanced right and left and headed in the direction of an alleyway. Lizzy, Cory and Preston followed closely behind.

"This place feels evil," said Lizzy, her voice shaky.

"Look—at the end of this alley—there's a lean-to shelter. We will at least rest for a short time," said Eli. He carried Annie to the end where he gently set her down. Lizzy dropped to the pavement and cradled Annie's head in her lap. Annie moaned softly and again pulled her sore arm close to her body.

Lizzy and the boys hovered over Eli, looking around uneasily. "It feels like we're being watched," said Preston. "I don't like it here."

"Annie must be conscious before we start again," said Eli. "She appears to be experiencing shock. Preston, you and Cory carry that metal sheet over here so we will be more protected and out of sight. Be as silent as possible."

The boys obeyed Eli's order and carried a large panel of sheet metal to the lean-to, enclosing the make-shift shelter from the street side. They placed it as silently as they could but it banged noisily as it touched the line of the roof. Once it was in place, Lizzy, Cory and Preston slid quietly into the shelter behind the spot where Annie lay.

"Is she going to be all right?" asked Lizzy.

"I will examine her arm," stated Eli. He pulled a pen-like object from his waistband. When he flicked it, a soft light shone from one end. Rolling up Annie's sleeve, he pointed the light at the crook of her arm. Eli frowned. "The delirium injection has become seriously infected. I fear blood poisoning has set in."

At that moment, Annie tried to jerk her arm free. As she did, she cried out in pain as her body shuddered. Sweat and tears rolled off her face and Eli pressed his hand against her forehead.

"She is burning with fever," Eli said solemnly. "Preston, I need the handbag."

Preston reached for the bag and handed it to Eli. Reaching deep inside, Eli pulled out the little fur-ball form of Timna. Holding the creature in the palm of his hand, he spoke softly to her in a language no one understood. Then, he placed Timna in the crook of Annie's inflamed arm. "Now, we must wait," he whispered.

"What was that?" asked Cory.

"I heard it, too," whispered Preston.

Just then, footsteps grated on the gravel of the alleyway and voices intermingled with shouts and lewd swearing. Instantly, several pair of hands grabbed the metal sheet and pulled it to the ground with a bang that echoed through the skyscraper canyons beyond. Lizzy and the boys crouched in terror as they knelt by the unconscious Annie.

"Well, lookee here!" A tall, muscular young man stood before them. He had a small light not unlike the one Eli used moments before. In the eerie shadows, his dark hair stood on end above his head in a stiff, punkish style, its greased texture glossy in the dreary light. His face was tattooed as were his arms where they were bare below ragged shirtsleeves of a filthy gray material. Wide leather bands decorated his wrists and matched the one that encircled his neck like a dog collar.

"Whutta you hidin' there?" Another young hoodlum muscled his way to the front and struck a match, lighting a cigarette held tightly between his crooked teeth. He, too, was covered with bizarre tattoos and leather armbands. He reached up to scratch his shaved head. "Hey, you slaves—get up 'ere and get a good look at this. You won't be seein' this any day soon." He pointed his finger directly at Lizzy. As he pointed, five or six members of their gang came forward to leer at her. Their faces were full of curiosity and lust. "Hey, Bane, it sure 'nough is a girl." He addressed the man with the spiked hair, apparently the leader of the group.

"You dork! Of course, it's a girl and it looks like she's got her some real nice bodyguards," said Bane. He spoke slowly and stalked around the end of the lean-to, sizing up the situation for all its possibilities. "Now, the question is how to get 'em to the Cranny without a lot of fuss."

"And, without Lurch gettin' wind of it. I guess we could just finish 'em off right here and now."

Cory moved closer to Eli and whispered. "Now would be a good time to do that glow-y thing you did back at the Fed building."

"I may be forced to deploy another method," replied Eli.

Bane moved toward Eli. "Hey, big guy, move away from the girl." At that moment, Annie stirred and groaned in pain. Instead of moving away from Annie, Eli lifted her from the ground and motioned for Cory to follow him. "Take care of her—over there," he ordered. Cory lifted Annie in his arms and placed her into a corner of the dark alleyway.

"You gotta a big problem!" shouted Bane at Eli. He crouched low in an attack position. While the other members of the gang stood watching, Bane lunged at Eli with a knife. Instantly, Eli's right hand clamped tightly onto Bane's wrist and squeezed. When Bane dropped the knife, Eli cleanly caught it in mid-air. Eli's other arm curled around Bane's neck and the shining knife found its way to within an inch of his jugular. Bane was taller and somewhat heavier than Eli, yet Eli clearly had the upper hand in the struggle. Bane began thrashing but stopped when he felt the cold steel of the knife against his throat.

"You will order your gang to retreat!" shouted Eli. "Now!"

Bane struggled and the razor edge of the knife began to slit the skin under his chin. Drops of blood trickled down Bane's neck. "All right! Pug get 'em out of the alley!"

The gang member with the shaved head answered. "But, Boss, there's only one of him!"

"Get movin', Pug! He's drawin' blood!"

"Retreat immediately or your leader will die!" shouted Eli.

The gang, led by Pug slowly began to pull back into the blackness of the alley. They inched so slowly that Eli applied more pressure to the knife. More blood trickled down Bane's neck onto the dirty leather collar.

"Get *movin*' I tell ya!" shouted Bane.

Pug and the others turned and disappeared into the alley, leaving Eli with the knife still at Bane's throat.

"Lemme go—you made your point!" sneered Bane.

"Only if I have your word that you will leave us alone," answered Eli.

"We'll leave you alone!"

Eli was about to lower the knife when he heard a sound above his head. He turned sharply in time to see another of the gang members standing on a ledge above the lean-to. The man jumped down on Eli, pushing Bane to the side and sending the knife flying into the shadows. Instantly, the gang that had just disappeared returned to the fight scene like a pack of wolves. Bane got to his feet, his hand massaging the fresh cut to his throat.

"Nice work, Warp. You just saved yourself from your nightly beating." Bane resumed his former stance of stalking the area around Eli. His face twisted in demented hatred. He wiped the blood from his neck, contemplating his next step. When a gang member retrieved his knife, Bane stuck it securely in his belt. "You're gonna wish you'd never been born, big guy."

Cory, Preston and Lizzy watched the scene from the corner of the alley, their faces ashen with terror. They watched as Eli stood tall and defiant. Bane took a step toward Eli when suddenly an intense white light flooded the darkened alleyway. For a moment, no one could see anything; but, in seconds, there appeared at least ten men in dark clothing surrounding the gang members. The light temporarily disarmed the gang, but when the darkness returned, they attacked the newcomers with ferocious battle cries.

"Get 'em! Drag 'em down to the river!" shouted Bane. His hand wielded his knife and as he raised it against Eli, the blade began to burn with a red luster. When the red light reached the metal in the handle, Bane screamed. The knife hit the pavement with a metallic thud. "What the—!" yelled Bane. He grabbed Eli by the throat but with an effortless twist, Eli was out of his grasp and had him in a grip that sent Bane to his knees screaming for mercy.

Eli punched him and sent him flying into the brick wall of the nearest building. Then, Eli turned to Lizzy and the boys who were still huddled in the corner by Annie. "Stay there!" he shouted. Eli looked up to see the men who had come seemingly out of nowhere engaged in hand-to-hand combat with the gang members. The street gang fought like animals, snarling and barring their teeth. The one called Pug was pounding on one of the newcomers. He had just drawn a sharp object out of his jacket when Eli observed the same phenomenon—the metal object glowed red and became too hot to hold. It fell to the ground and Pug's opponent flattened him, knocking him unconscious.

Just then, a punch came out of nowhere and sent Eli into the brick wall. Eli got up, ran his fingers through his hair and returned the blow. It was the man called Warp and he wasn't giving up easily. He was four inches taller than Eli and outweighed him by thirty pounds. He had recovered from Eli's shot and came at a running charge, grabbing Eli by the waist. Eli pulled off Warp's grip and with one mighty heave, tossed him twenty feet into a pile of trash cans. Warp got to his feet, somewhat dazed and charged again at Eli. He hit him full force but Eli deflected the impact. Turning to Warp, Eli delivered a sharp upper cut to the man's chin and sent him unconscious to the pavement.

Eli took stock of the fight and saw that the gang members were losing miserably. These newcomers dressed in dark uniforms were organized and skillful in hand-to-hand combat. The last of the gang members was being pounded; and, after screaming for mercy, was sent off into the night.

"We've got to get you out of here," said a low voice from behind. Eli swung around to see a middle-aged man approaching. "My name is Winger. You can trust us—we're with the Reserve."

"The Reserve?"

"The underground—the resistance movement." Winger looked around cautiously. "We need to move—get to the Harbor before more of them come back—believe me that was child's play compared to what it could be. Let's go!" Winger shouted orders to his men.

Eli looked the man over. There was no time to argue and he had no choice but to trust Winger. His men had saved their lives and he needed no more proof than that.

One of the men helped Annie to her feet. Annie was pale and weak and it took two men to help her along.

"Wait just a moment," ordered Eli. The men stopped while Eli checked Annie's arm. He pulled Timna away and placed the little animal in the pocket of his shirt. "All right—let us go."

Cory and Preston followed the men as they filed through a hole in the wall behind the lean-to. Eli grabbed Annie's bag and, taking Lizzy by the hand, followed behind the boys.

The group emerged from the alley onto a street cluttered with garbage and heaps of twisted metal. Buses were on their sides with windows broken out and tires punctured and burned.

They moved quickly along the sidewalks past more vacant stores with shattered windows. In the distance, they could see people huddled around fires cooking food. Dead animals littered the gutters and the stench made Cory and Preston cough.

"Miss Dibble, how are you doing?" asked Eli. He and Lizzy walked quickly alongside the men who were helping her along.

"Eli, I feel like I'm going to faint again," she whispered.

"We've got to move faster!" urged Winger. "Another group could jump us any moment!"

"Allow me to take Miss Dibble, Mr. Winger," offered Eli. He didn't wait for permission but swooped Annie up in his arms and began a slow sprint behind the men. "Lead the way, sir. Cory and Preston, help Lizzy! And keep up!"

The small band wound their way through the streets and alleyways. The street bonfires slipped behind them and soon the smell of the river replaced the foul stench of the inner city.

"Where do we go from here, sir?" asked Eli as he turned to Winger.

"We go under—each of my men has a breathing device and knows the way perfectly. It's a clean dive to the underwater entrance. Won't take more than twenty minutes. C'mon—we'll help you."

"But, sir, we have children here and one of them is gravely ill," replied Eli.

"I can see that—you can continue to help the miss there. Just share a breathing mask and follow the orange light once you're submerged. Now let's go!" Winger immediately entered the water off the grassy embankment, put the mask on and was underwater. An orange orb began to glow and descend under the shiny surface.

One of the resistance men handed Lizzy, Cory, and Preston each a breathing mask. "There's no trick to using this—just breath. There's a strap to keep it in place." He worked his way over to Eli and put a mask over Eli's face. "We don't have enough for everyone—just had a few extras while we were on patrol."

"I will share with Miss Dibble—lead the way," replied Eli.

"But, what about Timna?" asked Annie weakly.

"She is an arphax, Miss Dibble. They have been known to hold their breath for over an hour. There is no need to worry about her."

One by one, the men of the Reserve submerged themselves in the river and disappeared beneath the dark waters. Lizzy, Cory, and Preston followed with Eli close behind.

"Take a deep breath, Miss Dibble—we are going underwater. I will share the oxygen mask—trust me."

Annie, secure in Eli's arms, nodded and leaned her head against him wearily. The orange orb marked the path and he swam toward it. Annie clung to his form as his arms pulled in strong strokes toward the underwater procession. Stopping every few minutes to share the breathing mask, Eli checked to see if Annie was still conscious. He could dimly make out the forms of Lizzy, Cory, and Preston through the dingy water up ahead.

The orange orb led them around the wharves and around sunken boats. Cement pilings and other rubble at times blocked their way but still on went the orange orb over and around until finally they came to an outcropping of huge boulders. Eli and the others followed the orange light around and through the boulders until finally another light shone in the distance. As they drew closer, they could see it was a gigantic round doorway and it took its circular shape from the evenly spaced blue lights that lit its border.

Winger, still holding the orange orb, swam ahead of the others and touched a panel on the rock wall. Immediately, the door split into two huge halves, bisecting vertically in the middle. Winger motioned with the light to follow him into the chamber after the doors had receded. Eli and Annie were the last to enter and, as they passed through the opening, the massive metal doorway moved back to its closed position. They hung there, suspended, until the sound of rushing water reached their ears. The water was draining from the chamber. As soon as there was air to breathe, everyone removed their breathing mask and gasped.

"How is Annie?" asked Lizzy as she swam to Eli.

"We must get her to a quiet place as soon as possible," replied Eli solemnly.

The water drained completely and soon they were standing there shivering on a smooth paved surface. The chamber was empty of anything but the metal outside doorway to the river and a small door to the side. Winger went to another panel by the small door and pushed a button.

"We're ready to exit," he stated into the intercom.

"Yes, Winger. I'm coming to meet you myself."

Winger stood by the small door as he looked at his men. "Well, you're a motley crew to look at but I want to commend you on a job well done! Our patrol tonight was a success! Now let's get into some dry clothes!" He turned to Eli. "We'll see that the girl gets some medical attention." He turned back to the door when he heard footsteps on the other side.

The door buzzed and then flew open as a young man burst into the room. Annie looked up weakly from Eli's arms. She didn't think the man looked much older than she. He was of medium height and weight and wore brown corduroy pants and a navy blue tee shirt. His thick, dark-rimmed glasses magnified his blue eyes and he smiled as he extended his hand to Eli. "Welcome to the Harbor. I'm Nicolas Wycliffe."

Fifteen

Jack's jaw dropped as he read the sign on the office door, "Commander One, Jack Flint." Twenty minutes before, he had been summoned by intercom to meet Com Two at the armory. Slipping out of his dormitory room, Jack had gone down several hallways looking for the elevators. Apparently, taking a wrong turn, he found himself walking down an unfamiliar corridor and stopped abruptly when he saw the sign on an office door.

Jack glanced in both directions of the hallway. Then, he saw the door stood ajar; a cleaning lady was intent on her work dusting and vacuuming. Jack entered the office and the woman looked up.

"Excuse me . . . I'm wondering if I may . . . if I—"

"Mr. Flint—if you're wanting to see this office, well . . . what could be wrong about that?" The woman smiled and patted him on the arm as she left the room, leaving the door open a crack.

Jack stood staring after her. It seemed that everyone knew who he was or maybe more correctly, who he would someday be. He gently closed the door and turned to face the room. Why did he feel as though he were intruding, trespassing? After all, this was *his* office, wasn't it? He saw that it was not unlike Com Two's —a large desk dominating the far end by a row of windows which overlooked the parade grounds, a gargantuan television screen on the west wall, and shelves full of books, mementoes, and pictures. Yes, his name was on the door, but he couldn't have felt more strangely than if he had been in the Oval Office.

Jack walked slowly to the bookcase which stood against the wall opposite the television. The books ranged from Shakespeare's classics to technical books on unfamiliar subjects to volumes from all the world's religions. Then, his eyes fell to a picture, one with which Jack was familiar. It was his family gathered by a pristine lake high in the Teton Mountains. In fact, the picture had just been taken the week before—the week before he had been timesnatched. But, it looked old, yellowed, and crinkly behind the glass frame. He picked it up and studied the faces that now seemed years away. Did they miss him? Did they even know that he had disappeared?

On the shelf next to the picture, Jack saw an award of some kind. It was a crystal Polaris, the pole star, and had gold metallic lettering on the lower edge which read, "Coalition of Liberty Medal of Honor." Underneath, it said "Commander One, Jack Flint." Jack picked up the award and marveled. It was solid and heavy. He wondered what Com One had done to merit the honor. What future deed would he do to earn an award of this precedence? Whatever the accomplishment, he felt sure that there were light years of preparation ahead of him.

Jack was about to leave when he saw a collage of pictures in a large frame on the wall by the windows. He walked slowly to the collection of photographs and when he looked them over, he gasped. There in the middle of the frame was one that was larger than the others. It had been taken on the tarmac and the backdrop was a heliplane with the Pole Star symbol. In it, Commander One, Jack Flint, was dressed in the Coalition uniform and beret. He was standing with a group of soldiers and they were all laughing and seemed to be celebrating something. And to Com One's right, linked arm in arm, was Capt. Garcia.

"Garcia?" mouthed Jack to himself, frowning. "We're going to be good friends? Buddies?" The thought seemed absurd.

Jack took a deep breath and gazed at the rest of the pictures. They were mostly snapshots of Com One in uniform with his friends. All the pictures were taken on tarmacs or near military equipment. He was about to look away when another picture caught his attention. It was in the lower right corner and it was of Annie, older and more mature. Jack studied the photograph. She was dressed in a flowing summer dress; her hair was in a thick braid which fell down her back; and she was caught up in a close embrace in Com One's arms. Jack quickly looked away, confused. What did the future hold for him? Had all this time travel created or destroyed the scenes these pictures portrayed? The photographs brought into his mind a million questions. How could he find the answers? He frowned because he didn't know. Then, turning swiftly on his heel, he exited the room, carefully leaving the door open a crack, just as the cleaning lady had left it.

***

"You are each being issued a chronometer. You will notice that the back dials indicate the coordinates of our physical destination and the corresponding time destination." Capt. Garcia glanced up from his briefing to see that everyone was paying attention.

Jack flipped the gold chronometer over in his hand. It was the same one he used in Tel Aviv. He ran his finger over the lines of the embossed Pole Star on the front of the machine. He knew the location dials were set for the heart of Manhattan, somewhere around Central Park. He was told the chronometer wouldn't transport them there, but would tell them the physical location of their time destination. They would board the heliplane and be over the North American continent in two hours or less. His gaze fell to the time dials—they read 0800, 8-15-2036. So, they would be going back a day in time to hopefully meet up with Eli and Annie—the right Eli and Annie, the ones in the right time level. Lt. Shaw and her crew determined that the dials stopping at these coordinates was an unmistakable signal indicating Annie's location. Jack shook his head and sighed. He would leave those conclusions to the experts—to him it was all so confusing.

"You will be ready at 0500 hours tomorrow, 16 August 2036. Is that understood?" Garcia glanced over the group which consisted of Jack, Cpl. White, Lt. Parrish and Sgt. Skeen who were both on the first rescue mission in New York.

"Yes, sir," they answered in unison.

Twenty minutes later, Jack was back in his dorm room. He slipped the chronometer into his front pocket and began filling his bag with the issued clothing he had been given at the base. He threw in his extra pair of PT clothes and smiled. Maybe there would be a chance to run in Central Park. That is—after the rescue. He had seen pictures of the huge green expanse of Central Park with its lakes and running paths. He would relish a few moments there after they got Annie and Eli out of the clutches of General Graff and Finke.

Jack's eyes fell to the handgun lying on the bed. Garcia was adamantly against giving Jack a weapon, but the weapons range director showed him the targets—proof of Jack's abilities. The director had told Garcia he would be crazy not having every member of the team armed. Jack could see that it still stuck in Garcia's throat that Jack was going at all.

A knock came at the door.

"Come in."

Cpl. White peered around the corner of the door. "I have something for you, sir."

"Come in—and, you don't have to call me 'Sir'—I don't think I'm much older than you are."

"It's in my training, Com One. I mean, I can't help it, sir."

"Yeah, I guess," replied Jack. "What's that you're carrying?"

"It's a utility belt. They're pretty much standard issue."

"Let's see it, then."

White threw the belt on the bed and set a small bag on the floor. The belt was about two inches wide and made of nylon mesh, the same color as the Coalition uniform. It included a holster for a weapon and had some carabiners attached at intervals. A small round case was at the front.

"This is a life-saver," said White as he reached for the round case. He flipped open a snap on the front and began pulling out a thin rope. "There was nothing like *this* twenty years ago—it's tested at over 2,000 pounds. It pulls out effortlessly and automatically rewinds itself in three seconds."

White then unsnapped a six-inch long case. He pulled out a sleek, black knife and handed it to Jack. "If you ever have to cut that rope, this is the only knife around that can do it. It's edged with a diamond coating." White looked at Jack with a smile. "And, if you need it to go back together, the rope will adhere to itself like a magnet. And, it'll be just as strong as before it was cut, maybe stronger."

Jack took the rope in his hand. "Amazing."

"Go ahead—try it."

Jack looped the rope in his hand and cut it with the knife. Then, he looked at Cpl. White.

"Just get the two ends close to each other and they'll reattach."

Jack took one end of the rope and as he passed it by the other cut end, the two ends drew together and fused

"See what I mean?"

"Wow. Is the knife good for other stuff?"

"Yeah, in fact, be aware that it'll cut through most anything, especially a finger—so be careful with it," answered White.

"Right. So, what's this?"

"A flashlight that has a range of 100 yards. It could light up the scoreboard at your favorite football game from one of the end zones. You gotta use some precaution with it. Don't worry—you'll get used to it."

Jack picked up the belt with a puzzled look on his face. "Where's the buckle—how do you fasten this thing?"

White reached over and slipped the belt around his own waist. Instantly, the belt did the same thing as the rope—it fused together so perfectly that Jack couldn't see where it joined.

"That's quite an invention."

"Yeah, I think it came from the space program before it got cancelled—the astronauts got tired of fumbling to fasten things in outer space, so someone came up with this instant fusing process. Lots of apps for it."

"So, what's in the bag?" asked Jack, pointing to the bag White had set on the floor.

"Oh, that's your uniform." White pulled a dark green Coalition uniform from the bag and handed it to Jack. "That's what we'll all be wearing tomorrow. If it doesn't fit, I'll take you down to clothing supply."

Jack slipped on the shirt, pants and cap. They fit perfectly. Running his hand over the Coalition symbol, the Pole Star, he looked at White. "It's an honor to wear this."

"Yeah, I feel the same way. Well, I'd better go—we need to get some rest. Oh-five-hundred comes pretty early."

***

The thunderous beating of the heliplane rotors shook the tarmac as the Coalition team boarded the aircraft the next morning in the early morning dusk. A mild wind was sweeping over the mountaintops and the star shine reflected off the surface of the fjord below the base. Stowing their baggage, the five men took their seats and readied themselves for the flight to New York City. Jack took a seat near the back next to Skeen.

"I don't think I'll ever get used to this thing," said Jack.

"I know what you mean—hey, look who's joining us."

Jack looked up to see Commander Two, Ethan Dibble, enter the heliplane. He was dressed in the Coalition uniform with a sidearm in a black leather holster. He nodded his greetings to the Coalition team members and took a seat at the front.

"I'm glad he's joining us," said Skeen. "He didn't get to be Com Two for nothing. He's been on some pretty horrendous missions. It doesn't surprise me that he's coming along—I mean, seeing that his daughter is part of the reason we're going."

"Yeah, I don't blame him," replied Jack. Relief at the sight of Com Two washed over him. He hated the thought of being on a mission commanded by Garcia. Dibble's presence might temper Garcia's attitude toward him. At least he hoped so.

The door was closed; and, as everyone prepared for take-off, Jack could feel the powerful beating of the massive rotors as the heliplane lifted off the Norwegian soil. It was too dark to see anything out the windows except the lights of the base as they disappeared beneath them. The dark, open sea lay ahead and, before they had reached the coastline, the metal plating covered the windows and the engines shot them into hypersonic speed toward North America.

"Okay, listen up." It was the voice of Capt. Garcia over the loudspeaker. "Now that we're in the air, it's briefing time."

Jack sat up in his seat and leaned forward with his elbows on his knees.

"Intel sources have given us the all-clear on landing at the eastern end of Central Park. The Fed patrol will be gone by our ETA and we'll just have scrappers to deal with. Don't underestimate them."

Jack raised his hand.

Garcia nodded in his direction.

"Sir, what's a 'scrapper'?"

"We're talking about the human dregs that are roaming the streets of New York. They've taken over the city—divided into gangs. Even the Feds avoid them." Garcia looked over the group. "Any other questions?" No one responded. "Okay, the chronometers can't transport us to our destination so we'll have to stick to the coordinates like glue. I'll head up the operation, so stay close behind." Garcia's voice softened. "Com Two, are you okay with bringing up the rear?"

"Certainly," replied Dibble.

"All right then. Parrish, you're after me, then Skeen, Flint, and White followed by Com Two. Is that clear?"

"Yes, sir."

"We'll exit the chopper and make for the coordinates. We'll call for the chopper when the mission is accomplished. Everyone will be issued an AKS upon departure. Keep alert—I can't overemphasize the threat in the inner city. Expect trouble around every trash can. We'll arrive at the coordinates, then punch in the time destination. That should do it. Any questions?" No one answered so Garcia sat down.

Jack sat back in his seat and turned to Skeen. Sgt. Skeen was a big man in his mid-thirties. Jack thought he would be a good candidate for a Navy Seal team. Skeen was in top physical condition and the morning before had beaten Jack to the top of the mountain by half an hour. "So, when did the 'scrappers' take over New York?" asked Jack.

"About eight years ago—when the Federation kinda gave up on the city. You ever been to New York?"

"Just the time you guys rescued me. Didn't see much."

"Well, you won't recognize it. There was a huge war that took place there in about '24. Most everyone migrated to outlying areas. Except for the scrappers—they live underground and forage for themselves. I guess the Fed doesn't think they're much of a threat or they'd exterminate 'em."

"If Miss Dibble and Eli are in the city, how will they survive?" asked Jack, his brow furrowed.

"Flint, she'll just have to rely on Eli's abilities."

Jack looked puzzled.

"Some things are classified, but I can tell you I've seen him in action." Skeen grinned widely and lowered his voice. "Man, you ain't seen nothing like it. He can throw a 200-pound man like he was a sack of spuds. He's light on his feet and has more endurance than anyone I've ever seen. If you're worried about Miss Dibble, don't be—he's also very smart and figures things out. Great tactical mind. We'll find 'em all right."

Jack couldn't deny that Skeen's remarks made him feel better. He sunk back into the soft leather seat. He had been up most of the night wired and overanxious. Three hours before he was due to wake up, he had fallen asleep. The steady hum of the plane's engines soothed his nerves and he found himself closing his eyes. The muscles of his face and back slowly began to relax. Soon, he was in a dreamlike state almost at the point of deep sleep when a picture came into his mind of Annie. She was sunken in deep, murky water and her long hair was floating around her face. Her skin was ashen and gaunt and she was limp in someone's arms.

A round, orange light was floating beside her and it was moving. Everything was moving; the water, Annie, the light and arms—arms that were pulling at the water in long graceful movements.

Then, the flash of a knife blade made the scene vanish and Jack could see blood trickling down a neck. Was it Annie's? Was it Eli's? Were they in the hands of the scrappers? Jack jerked awake. His heart was pounding and sweat was forming on his brow. He looked around at the others but most of them were sleeping. He glanced to the front at Com Two who was reading a small book.

Jack unbuckled his seat and went to the front. "Sir, may I speak with you a moment?"

"Sit down, Jack," invited Com Two. "What is it?"

"I'm going to do the best I can to follow orders, sir, but I keep having these premonitions or visions. I can't seem to help it. But, every time I have them, they come true."

"What's the latest one?" Com Two dog-eared the page he had been reading.

"I just saw Annie, sir—she was underwater and didn't look good at all. And, then . . I . . ."

"Spit it out, Jack."

"It looked like someone was getting their throat cut." Jack looked down at his feet.

"I've heard a number of time signature accounts, Jack. I believe they are glimpses into the past or future."

"That's just it, sir—I wouldn't know if those things have already happened or not."

"Well, we're too far removed from it to do anything about it. I think we ought to take things as they come and be prepared for the worst. Going it alone never works out very well, I'm afraid."

"I know you're right, sir. I just thought you ought to know what I saw."

"Thank you—I appreciate that, Jack. Now, let's concentrate on being a cohesive unit and not going off half-cocked." Dibble reopened his book, a clear sign that the conversation was over.

***

Jack could feel the heliplane descending and slowing. When the metal plates over the windows retracted, it was a sure indication that they were close to New York. He got up and took a window seat just in time to see the plane's wing pull back toward the fuselage and for the rotors to begin their rhythmic beat.

Peering through the window, Jack could see the unmistakable skyline of the city. But, there was something different, something unfamiliar from the many pictures he had seen in magazines and on television, something he hadn't noticed the day they escaped from the old United Nations building. There was something dull and dead about the scene before him. He searched in vain for the Statue of Liberty and figured he was at the wrong angle. The skyscrapers reached toward the heavens, as always, but their windows didn't reflect the sunshine as he would have expected. They drew nearer and, to Jack's astonishment, there were hundreds, maybe thousands of windows blown out of most of the buildings and large black marks were on the walls of the lower levels.

The lower they flew, the more apparent it became that New York City had at some time been a war zone. He wasn't familiar enough with the area to know the names, but Jack could see a massive bridge which had collapsed into the river and the vegetation and trees were burned and charred. He saw no signs of life, no traffic either on the roads or on the waterways.

Jack frowned. What had happened here? What had happened to one of the most populated and major cities in the world? As they drew closer to Central Park all thoughts of spending a leisurely afternoon exploring its pathways disappeared. It was gray, dead, and destroyed.

Jack looked over at Skeen who returned his questioning gaze with a look, a knowing look as if he knew exactly what Jack was thinking. Jack looked back out the window. New York City was dead. New York City was no more. And more importantly to him, Annie Dibble was somewhere down there. Was she alive? The lower they descended the more he felt his hope fading. Annie was down there—she was somewhere down there in all the destruction. Somewhere down there among the scrappers, among the rubble, and maybe fighting for her life.

Sixteen

"No, Miss Dibble, you are not hallucinating—that was back in the detention cell of the Federation building."

"But, my arm—Eli. It's completely healed. There isn't even a trace of the injection hole." Annie Dibble sat on an overstuffed sofa in what seemed to be a storage room for foodstuffs and bedding.

"Due to the talents of the little arphax, Timna," Eli replied. There was a trace of satisfaction in his voice.

"But, how could *she* make my arm well?"

"Let me explain. The great civilization from which I originate has discovered many advanced technologies. When it came time to travel the cosmos, we took with us many means to divert disease and maladies discovered by our scientists and physicians. However, even as advanced as our society had become, our space travelers were wont to take along a centuries-old, tried-and-true method of healing—the arphax. Just how long the arphax has been a part of our culture cannot be determined."

"But, *how* did she do it?" Annie ran her hand over the skin where the needle had punctured her vein. It had been swollen, red, streaked and feverish the last time she saw it. The fire in her arm had been enough to make her faint. Now, it was smooth and soft with no blemish whatsoever. In addition, after Annie regained consciousness, she never felt better in her life.

"We may never know—after all, she cannot speak," answered Eli.

"What a marvelous little creature." Annie reached for Timna who had been resting in the palm of Eli's hand. "You dear little thing. I owe you my life."

"As do I. I would not be here if it were not for Timna. She has been indispensable to me during my mission here on your planet."

"You call it a mission—then, you someday plan to depart?"

"When I can no longer be of service to Commander One, I will return to my people."

"Why Commander One?"

"When I first arrived here, it was he who impressed me to stay. He told me of the work of independence with which I could seriously aid him. He convinced me that I could be of invaluable service. And, your—"

114

"Yes, go on."

"Your words—I mean the words of the future Annie Dibble—also persuaded me to stay longer and to contribute to the cause of liberty."

Annie blushed and turned back to Timna. She stroked the little animal between her eyes and patted her tiny paw. "I had no idea."

"Of course not, Miss Dibble. How could you?"

"Eli, may I ask you a question?"

"Please do."

"When we first met you— I mean, when Jack and I first encountered you at Federation headquarters you decided to stay and retreat another way. Somehow did you fear the Federation? I mean, you have amazing abilities and could have escaped any time you wanted."

"I can see why you are confused on this point, Miss Dibble," replied Eli. He shifted his position in the lounge chair in which he sat and glanced at the door. Then, he lowered his voice. "You see, I became an invaluable informant for the Coalition while I had infiltrated the Federation. I had gained the complete confidence of General Graff. I had the means of supplying the Coalition with a goodly amount of intelligence during my time there. But, eventually Com One informed me I was of more use to them back at Pole Star. It was about that time that a complication presented itself." Eli stopped to clear his throat. He raked his hair with his fingers and shifted his position again. "I planned to retreat with the Coalition; but, as I was saying, a complication ensued that I was not counting on. Actually—"

"Was the complication Lizzy?"

Eli looked at Annie for a long moment. "Yes. In my life I had never experienced the kinds of feelings I encountered when I first saw her. My entire soul rebelled at the thought of her being any kind of slave to General Graff. I learned that Lizzy was not in immediate danger but I read things into the way the General looked at her. I knew I had to do something; hence, the reason for my opting out of joining the rescue mission. I had to see Lizzy one more time to assure her that I would return for her in the future. Once I determined that she was safe, I communicated a rendezvous time with her. By returning to seek out Lizzy, I put myself and the mission in partial jeopardy."

"But, your strength and abilities . . ."

"Miss Dibble, I plainly have some superior skills, but I am not infallible—I am subject to death like anyone else."

Annie smiled. "So, you had planned on going back later to rescue Lizzy?"

"And, the other time children."

"Eli, do you realize that Lizzy is many years younger than you? I mean, she is only fifteen, just a child."

"I am aware of that fact. Of course, I will do as she wishes, but I am fully prepared to wait for her."

"Eli, do you know why Lizzy was timesnatched?"

"That is easy to determine. Lizzy is the very famous Elizabeth Coleman, a world-renowned singer and musician. General Graff has a penchant for fine music and that is why he took advantage of her musical abilities at the Federation. I was always watching out for her, making sure she was in no immediate peril."

Annie looked at Eli with new eyes. He seemed to have a depth of character rare among young men his age. But, then, she had to admit she wasn't aware what his true age was. He looked to be in his early twenties, but maybe he was far older on his world.

"Eli, you are a decent man."

"I thank you for your confidence, Miss Dibble."

Annie studied Eli's face for a moment. She admired his unassuming nature. His dark features were handsome by any standards but he was seemingly unaffected by that fact. She could see what an asset he was to Com One.

"Eli, you said your people had many advanced technologies. And, yet, you told me once that there were similarities to our people."

Eli nodded. "Yes, our civilization is what I would term 'enlightened.'" His eyes lifted toward the ceiling in deep thought. "It comes from our belief in a higher power. Many of your people are enlightened but many walk in darkness, not acknowledging their dependence on something greater than themselves."

"Then, you believe in God," said Annie softly.

"Yes, and that belief has propelled us to the singular advancement that we enjoy. Darkness equals fear which results in regression. Regression limits one's thinking, not only spiritually, but scientifically. There truly is no limit to the amount of progression a society can achieve, given that enlightened conditions are present. Our world has proven that many times over."

A knock came at the door which startled Annie. She sat up straight on the sofa and returned Timna to Eli.

"Come in," said Eli.

The door opened and in walked Cory and Preston. Right behind them entered the young man who had introduced himself the night before as Nicolas Wycliffe. He walked boldly up to Eli and Annie and drew up a chair.

"How is the arm, Miss Dibble?"

"As you can see, it's completely healed, Mr. Wycliffe." She turned her arm out so that he could clearly see the spot where the wound had been.

"But, I was told you were gravely ill and barely made it alive through the tunnel."

"That's true." Annie glanced at Eli, not knowing if he wanted to share the miracle of Timna.

Wycliffe furrowed his brow and grinned at the same time. "Well, it looks as though our Dr. Nelson is more talented than I had imagined."

"Mr. Wycliffe," stated Eli, "My little companion, Timna, was the means of Miss Dibble's recovery. She came with me from my world." Eli extended his hand where Timna lazily stretched her four extremities and gave a little shake.

Wycliffe's eyes grew wide and his mouth dropped open. "Why, I've never seen the likes of it! May I?" He gingerly extended his hand toward Timna.

Eli gently dropped Timna into the palm of Wycliffe's hand. She cuddled down into its warmth and retracted everything; eyes, ears, feet, and tail.

Wycliffe laughed. "What an extraordinary creature. Now what's this about 'your world'?"

Eli cleared his throat and gave a brief account of his intergalactic travels and his reasons for being in the employ of the Coalition.

"You'll have to forgive me, my friend. I'm rather new around here," admitted Wycliffe. "I find myself discovering new information on a daily basis. I suppose I shouldn't be surprised."

"Excuse me, Mr. Wycliffe, but I must ask—are you related to the Nicolas Wycliffe who invented the chronometer?" asked Annie.

"I am one and the same. It's a complicated tale and one I fully intend to reveal eventually. A brief synopsis will have to do for now. Indeed, I am credited with the invention of the chronometer. More accurately, I would say that I *discovered* the properties of chronomium and that only because of my grandfather."

"But, if I'm figuring right, you should be much older than you appear. Why, you don't seem to be much older than I," stated Annie.

"You're correct, Miss Dibble. Actually, I was quite minding my own business at home one day not long ago. Parenthetically, I might add that my home happens to be in Yorkshire. We live in a manor on the moors—very lonely—but very conducive to scientific study. You know—the long hours indoors whilst the wind rearranges the hills, or so it seems sometimes. At any rate, I was simply doing some experiments one day when all of a sudden—*whoosh.*"

"*Whoosh?*"

"Well, it was very sudden. You see, a tall gentleman in a long, blue coat appeared at my side and whisked me away to where we all find ourselves. I mean, in the present time level—2036."

"His name is Finke," said Annie. "Where did he take you?"

"To the middle of Central Park, actually. He indicated that he had made a mistake as to location and seemed rather flustered when immediately we were surrounded by the most scandalous-looking hoodlums I had ever seen in my life. Just at the moment of dire peril, I was rescued from not only the man you call Finke but from the gang of thieves which I am sure intended to cut my throat at the first opportunity."

Annie was absorbed by Wycliffe's account. His clear blue eyes danced with enthusiasm as he retold his experience. "Who rescued you?" she asked.

"The gentlemen of the Reserve who live here in the Harbor. They are led by James Winger. I believe you made his acquaintance in much the same way I did." Wycliffe smiled easily. His brown hair was thick and short and swept back in spite of an unruly cowlick.

"Excuse me, but I was told that chronometers don't transport physically, but just backward or forward in time," stated Annie.

"Yes, that's true," answered Wycliffe. "Older models lacked the capacity of transporting to any particular location. It seems the Federation did some experimenting of its own and stumbled upon a rudimentary form of physical transport. In my case, the man you call Finke over or under calculated the location; and, hence, our arrival in Central Park among the thieves."

"Well, there's no wondering why *you* were timesnatched," commented Annie.

"I suppose not," said Wycliffe. "But, why were you?"

"Well, when I grow up, I'm going to be a great writer and be the voice of freedom over Radio Free America." Annie gave a little laugh as though the proposition were absurd. "I was also taken the same time as Jack Flint."

Wycliffe said nothing.

"Jack Flint is also known as Commander One of the Coalition. But, to me, he's just a kid who, like me, got caught up in a most fantastical set of circumstances."

"Yes, I believe Winger has mentioned this 'Com One' a time or two. And, how is it that you're separated?"

"Well, we were on a mission of sorts to save our future selves from being killed when Eli and I were timesnatched again from the same scoundrel Finke. Jack was left behind to wonder what in the world became of us." Annie looked down at the floor, clearly saddened at the thought.

"Oh, dear," said Wycliffe. "That means you are on different time levels. Let's see, I would calculate that you are on time level four and your friend Jack is on level two, if I'm not mistaken in my figures."

"Time level four?"

"I discovered the complication of time levels when I tried to rescue my grandfather several years ago. It's a complicated tale—one for another day. Suffice it to say that the farther we go mixing up time levels, the more intricate a web we create—it can be most difficult to unwind it all."

Annie bit her lip and looked away.

"But, not to fear, Miss Dibble—even this very day I have discovered information— clues that will aid us with our dilemma. I'm at present working on the complexities of not only time transport but what I call 'location transport.' With an intricate GPS system incorporating time coding, which I have invented, I believe we shall be able to connect with other time levels." He stopped to see if Annie was following his conversation. "But, this is much too much so soon after your horrendous trip to the Harbor. Let's break for a bite to eat and then we'll put our heads together and come up with some solutions."

Annie looked into Wycliffe's eyes. She couldn't help but find Nicolas Wycliffe's cheery attitude uplifting. She smiled and followed as Wycliffe led everyone from the room out into a large area filled with more overstuffed sofas and chairs.

The floors were covered with carpet scraps laid out in a hodge-podge of colors and textures. The walls were strewn with shelves containing books and old vases and nick nacks. One shelf contained a variety of bottles of every size and shape and another was laden with canned food. A basket in one corner held nothing but boxes of matches. And, off in the corner by a lit Christmas tree was a table where Lizzy, Cory and Preston were eating something from a box.

"It's not the Ritz, but we get along pretty well," said Wycliffe. He led them to the table where Eli immediately took a seat next to Lizzy. "Please help yourself to the cuisine. It's an adventure every day to see what Ralph will dish up next." A plump man in the corner lifted his head from the boxes he was rearranging. He managed a wave of his hand and then went back to work.

Annie set her handbag at her feet and examined what the others were eating. The box contained cookies and there were containers of juice with straws. A loaf of bread was wrapped in plastic with jars of peanut butter and jelly.

"Thank you, Mr. Wycliffe—but, how did you discover this place? How do you keep it secure from the villains we encountered last night?" asked Annie.

"It will be my pleasure to answer that and many other questions very soon. Have your fill and then I'll return to show you the rest of the complex. I believe you will be intrigued by what I have to show you." With that, Wycliffe exited through the same door they had entered.

**

Annie chomped on a peanut butter and jelly sandwich. So much had happened in the past twenty-four hours that she had trouble focusing on the moment. Only the morning before, she had suffered hallucination torture at the hands of the Federation. Next, she spent the night, first in the horrors of mid-town Manhattan and then beneath the waves of the East River, sharing a breathing mechanism with Eli. Then, the skin on her arm, inflamed with fever and blood poisoning suddenly looked like that of a new-born baby. The line between reality and dream was dim at best.

Annie looked up from her thoughts to see Lizzy staring at her. "Lizzy, how are you doing by now?" she asked.

"Everything has happened so fast and it's hard to make sense of things," replied Lizzy. "I just keep wondering how my family back home is doing. Did you say Gemma was crying over me?"

"She was practically inconsolable."

Lizzy smiled and shook her head. "What a strange turn of events—we had just quarreled before I disappeared. Oh, what I would give to set things straight."

"Don't worry—we'll get out of this somehow." Annie touched Lizzy's hand. "But, they won't believe a word of our story, will they?"

"Probably not—thanks, Annie. I'm so glad you're here."

The group consisting of Eli, Annie, Lizzy and the boys had finished their noon meal when James Winger insisted on escorting them around the complex. Annie judged him to be about forty years old and had an outdoors look to him, as though he would be at home on an African safari. He affectionately referred to the complex as 'the Harbor.' So far, it had the eclectic feel of a warehouse/clubhouse/homeless shelter. What they termed the kitchen was nothing more than a row of cupboards with a goodly supply of can openers. Most of their meals either came out of cans or packages. To Annie, everyone seemed grateful for what they had and the place had a cozy feel to it.

"Mr. Winger, may I ask you a question?" ventured Eli.

"Of course."

"We were fighting the scrappers and then there you were— you and your men in the midst of the fray."

"Yes, what about it?"

"I could not help but make an observation." Eli stood next to Winger. "The scrappers were about to slice us with their knives when the blades began to glow red and the scrappers dropped them. Obviously, they were too hot to hold."

"One of the several inventions Wycliffe has been able to concoct since he's been here."

"How exactly does it work, if I may ask?"

"You'll have to ask Nick the physics behind it but he gave each of us a control that he just attached conveniently to our patrol lights."

Winger reached into his pocket and displayed the long instrument he had used in the dark alleyway. "When you push this button, it sends some kind of frequency, I guess, to whatever metal object you're pointing it at. During the fight, I just pointed it at a knife and that's all I needed." Winger put his light away and patted the pocket with satisfaction.

"Intriguing," said Eli.

"Wouldn't go out without it."

"You said he had created other inventions?"

"I'll leave it to Nick to fill you in on the others—he might be keepin' 'em secret for all I know. Hope you understand."

"Of course," replied Eli.

Winger put up his hand to stop the group. "We'll have to suit up here. The next room we'll be going in is what's called the 'clean room.' Very important not to track dirt in." He pointed to several lockers which contained white jumpsuits and head coverings of various sizes. Everyone slipped one on and waited for Winger to give the go-ahead. He stood at a large metallic door with a blinking red light and pushed a button. When the red light turned green, he pushed a lever and the door swung open.

Blazing white lights greeted the visitors as they entered what appeared to be a laboratory of some kind. It couldn't have been more opposite from the homely shelter they had just left. The floors were gleaming white tile so shiny Annie feared she would slip on them. The walls were white as was the ceiling from which hung numerous brilliant light fixtures. There was very little furniture except for a modern computer console area about twenty feet away where Nicolas Wycliffe was busy at the keyboard. There was a fresh outdoor quality about the air and Annie took in a deep breath, suddenly revived.

"Miss Dibble, look," whispered Eli. He was gazing in the opposite direction from where Wycliffe worked at the computer.

Annie turned. Her lips parted in surprise. A bank of five huge video screens hung seemingly in midair. Instead of hanging in a two-dimensional line end to end, they curved like the spine of a snake. Each screen showed a scene playing as though it were a motion picture. The scenes were constantly changing on some screens while others replayed as if on rewind. And, every screen showed scenes from the past forty-eight hours of Annie's life.

"What is the meaning of all this?" asked Annie. She backed away from the images toward Wycliffe's desk.

"If you find it disturbing, I apologize but I'm gleaning much needed information. Let me show you." Wycliffe hovered over the computer console and his hands flew over the keyboard in a blur. "Now then, just keep watching and I'll show you what I mean."

Immediately, the scenes began to change and Annie recognized the landscape of Tel Aviv. There they were—the Coalition team—at the airport, being whisked away through the terminal. There was the black SUV with its passengers on their way to the restaurant. Then, the scene changed and Jack, Annie, Eli, and Garcia were leaving the vehicle and huddling together as Garcia instructed them on the chronometer. Then, the scene froze. Annie and Eli looked at Wycliffe to see what the matter was. Wycliffe was also looking at the big screens and mumbling to himself. Then, looking back and forth between the screen and the computer, he began again to type furiously on the keyboard.

"What is it, Mr. Wycliffe?" asked Eli.

Wycliffe kept mumbling to himself and put up his hand for silence. The moments ticked away but Annie never looked away from the screens. Then, as though looking through the zoom of a camera's eye, the scene focused in on the small group still huddling. It had zoomed in near the arm of Capt. Garcia.

"Confound it! Just move a little to the left!" shouted Wycliffe. He typed a few more words on the keyboard.

Then, in slow, digital jerks the motion resumed until Wycliffe shouted again. "Perfect! Right there!"

"Right where?" asked Annie.

"The chronometers! All four of them visible at once!"

"Why is that important?" asked Eli. He approached Wycliffe at the console.

"Because, I'm going to do a bit of adjusting. I need to magnify them slightly." He turned a blinking dial above the computer screen and his eyes narrowed. "That should be close. Now, I think that I've been able to capture the calibration of each chronometer." Wycliffe let out a shrill whistle. "Let's hope that does it!"

"Does what?" Annie's thoughts raced. What was all this about? What did these giant images of the Tel Aviv mission have to do with anything?

"All right, let me explain." Wycliffe left the console and stood before the five giant screens. "I just succeeded in locking in each chronometer's time calibration. That will allow me to manipulate the physical and time destinations."

"What's the purpose of that?" asked Annie.

"It will allow me to set destinations from here on these four particular chronometers." Wycliffe looked at Annie and Eli. "If you wish to be rescued from this time level by someone in a compatible time level, this capability is critical."

"So, you're setting those chronometers in order that those on the other end can find us?" Annie felt a surge of hope.

"That's exactly what I've done. When I'm ready to set the destinations, the dials on those machines will spin until they come to rest at the proper settings which I will input into the computer."

"But, the Federation took my chronometer and probably Eli's, too."

Eli nodded in agreement.

"Well, no matter. The other two will suffice," said Wycliffe.

"When will you set the destinations?" asked Annie.

"At this very moment, if you like."

"Yes, I would like that—I would very much like that." Annie felt a smile take over her face and she glanced at Eli. Though she had never seen him truly smile, his eyes sparkled and he nodded to her.

"Well, let's get to it, then!" Wycliffe returned to his computer and motioned for them to join him. Once again, he bent over the keyboard. His fingers again flew over the keys as he occasionally glanced at the video screens. Several minutes passed when finally, he leaned back in his chair and laughed. "It's done."

"What's so funny?" asked Cory.

"Well, I get a particular delight in imagining the looks on the faces of the Coalition team as they watch the dials of their chronometers spinning out of control for no apparent reason." Wycliffe rose from his chair, chuckling to himself.

"But, they won't know why they're spinning," said Cory.

"My dear boy, you underestimate the intellect of the Coalition—they'll have it figured out in time." He chuckled once more. "No pun intended."

Exactly at that instant, the walls, floors, and video screens of the laboratory shook violently as an explosion rocked the building. For a split second, everyone was frozen in place. Then, Wycliffe yelled at everyone to follow him to the double doors at the back of the lab. But, before they could move, the door through which they had entered the lab flew open. The kitchen helper, Ralph, stumbled through the doorway covered with blood and soot.

"Nick! The Feds have breached the southern doors! Alpha Plan is in effect!"

Seventeen

When Premier Ivan Molotov drew himself up to his full height of six-foot-five, lesser men remained silent. When he took a long drag on his cigar, his eyes narrowing, intimidation was usually complete.

"I presume the alien and the girl are now in the Incarceration Levels?" Molotov addressed General Horatio Graff. Molotov's close-set eyes were blue and piercing and his pointed nose was a sharp contrast to his round, pale face.

"I . . .I . . .actually, they *were* detained on Incarceration Level Three," replied General Graff who sat at his desk in the old United Nations building high above the East River. His hands were sweating.

"*Were?*"

"I had found some success with the girl, Miss Dibble. She would have cooperated even more fully if . . . if. . ."

"Go on." Molotov moved into the light. A scar ran from his right cheekbone to the point of his chin, sucking a portion of the flesh inward. It had been delivered by misplaced sword play. The man with whom he had been sparring was never heard from again. Molotov reached for a toothpick from the food tray to pick at his white, even teeth, his only perfect feature.

General Graff rose from his desk and walked slowly to the bay of windows overlooking the city. "I'll be honest with you, Premier Molotov—they escaped."

"I see." Molotov stood before the massive, beady-eyed elephant, studying its charging stance. His brow furrowed and he frowned. "Graff, I personally helped design this building's security system after the take-over. It has one of the most complex electronic sensory systems in the world. I find it impossible to believe that anyone could escape from the lower levels undetected."

"I confess that we underestimated the abilities of the alien, Premier."

"How so?" Molotov lit a cigar and relaxed on the leather couch.

"He neutralized the alarm system. Just how he did it is not clear."

"What about the security guards? Were they asleep?" Molotov was not smiling.

"The guards confronted them in the main lobby—there were actually five individuals who escaped. The guards' weapons were . . . useless against the alien, sir."

"And they escaped into the night I suppose."

"Yes—but, given the state of the City, I am certain their survival was impossible. That fact is so assured that our guards didn't even pursue them beyond the Federation perimeter zone."

"I see." Molotov puffed on his cigar. "Tell me about this character in your employ. Let's see . . . I believe his name is Finke. Yes, tell me why you continue to engage him when he let Nicolas Wycliffe slip through his fingers."

General Graff walked away from the windows and cleared his throat. "That is a matter with which I will personally deal today. The man acts before he thinks and—"

"Summon him now."

"Yes, Premier." Graff went to his desk and pushed a button with a trembling finger. "Send Robert Finke up immediately." Ten minutes passed. When a knock came at the huge double doors of Graff's office, Graff pushed another button on his desk, activating the doors. Standing there in his long, blue coat was Robert Finke. Molotov immediately stood and approached Finke who took a step backwards when the Premier drew near.

"Mr. Finke. I wanted Nicolas Wycliffe. I wanted him very much. Did you realize that?" asked Molotov.

"Yes, of course," answered Finke, looking up at the premier.

"Did you know that Wycliffe is perhaps the most brilliant mind in this century?"

"I was . . . I was not aware."

"Of course not. Brilliance of that nature is rare. Stupidity is more common." Molotov looked Finke up and down. "Much more common."

"I miscalculated the location coordinates and . . . and—"

"Let me see your chronometer."

Finke fumbled through his coat pockets. With shaking hands, he offered his machine to Molotov.

"Ah, it's a beauty, isn't it? Why, look at the engraving of the Federation seal—simply exquisite. I've heard that you flash the chronometer momentarily at your victim just at the time of abduction. Quite clever."

Molotov made a display of pocketing Finke's chronometer into his own jacket. "I actually would like to present you with a gift—a new chronometer." Molotov drew another from his pocket and chuckled. "Actually, it isn't new at all. In fact, it has a few defects—I rescued it out of the reject pile a few years ago just in case I found a use for it. It's mostly perfect, except it has no engraving as does yours." Molotov flipped the machine over in his hand. "You see it was just a prototype that is lacking in some details. I'm sure you won't mind if I exchange it for yours?"

Finke's mouth was a straight line. "Of course not, sir."

Molotov suddenly tossed the chronometer in Finke's direction, clicking the top dial as it left his hand. As Finke easily caught it, he instantly disappeared.

General Graff gasped. "Wh . . .Where did you send him?"

"Where he can never bumble an assignment again." Molotov retrieved Finke's chronometer from his jacket. "This really is quite splendid. I believe I will keep it for my own."

"Premier Molotov, I respectfully ask to what time destination you have sent Robert Finke."

"And, I respectfully tell you I wasn't keeping track of the coordinates. Suffice it to say that I am quite fond of this method of elimination. It has no equal. It is bloodless, humane, and . . . permanent."

General Graff stumbled on his way back to his desk where he sank into his chair and mumbled. "I am aware of this method of elimination. Robert didn't have his bohrium bracelet on. He told me this morning it had broken and was being repaired."

"Yes. Unfortunate for him." Molotov reached for a drink from the food tray. He sipped it as he approached Graff at the desk. "When I heard he was responsible for losing Wycliffe, I knew something had to be done. I don't believe Wycliffe is dead—I believe he resides somewhere in the bowels of New York City."

"Finke told me they materialized in Central Park and that he left Wycliffe to his own resources when they were accosted by the city hoodlums. No one unarmed could survive the gangs," replied Graff.

"You're right—no one could survive . . . except . . ." Molotov tossed his newly-acquired chronometer in the air and caught it again. "Except a mind as brilliant as Wycliffe. I have read every book he ever wrote and his research papers and projects. The man can practically invent something out of nothing. You've heard of his fame and abilities. We could have had him if Finke hadn't fumbled the ball. We could have had his excellent mind, had it to mold and transform into a tool for the Federation."

"Yes," agreed Graff. "But, he's lost to us now—what do you mean to do?"

"I mean to get him back." Molotov sighed. "And, I'll do it with or without your help. Of course, it would be infinitely better to have the help of the entire Federation force."

"I assure you we are at your command, Premier."

"Yes, yes, I know . . . I will tell you something I did not share with Finke." Molotov lowered his voice. "We have received some intelligence—some intelligence about the City. I will need all of your troops; we are going in."

"Going in?"

"Yes, we are going in to the depths of the City where I believe Wycliffe is hiding. Into its very depths." Molotov again stood before the charging elephant, studying the thing top to bottom. "Hideous display, I don't know why you keep it." Then, he strode over to Graff and put his face to within inches of the general's. "Incidentally, if you fail me again, I shall see to it that you never command so much as a garrison on the outer frontiers of Siberia." He laughed. "No, perhaps I will have you join your stooge, Finke." Molotov laughed louder. "Yes, yes, that would be infinitely more fitting."

***

The building shook again and Annie Dibble fell to her knees onto the shiny white tile of the Harbor computer room. Cory reached down to help her to her feet.

"Thanks, Cory, I'm all right," yelled Annie as she slung her handbag over her shoulder and ran.

"Keep up with me!" shouted Nicolas Wycliffe as he pushed open the double doors of the laboratory. The room beyond was dimly lit and full of generators and blinking lights. It was a utility room with large water pipes overhead with meters and dials. Annie, Eli, Lizzy, Cory, and Preston fled with Nicolas to a barrage of barrels and cement barricades lined up against the opposite wall. "To the blockade," shouted Wycliffe as if he were a commanding general. "Duck down behind the cement!"

In the instant Preston, who was bringing up the rear, disappeared behind the cement barriers, gunfire blasted from an overhead trapdoor. Wycliffe lifted his eyes. "Oh, dear."

"What is it?" asked Eli.

"We are not entirely fortified here." Wycliffe bit his lip. "But, I'll think of something."

"Well, what was 'Alpha Plan' supposed to be?" asked Eli.

"Do you see that stairwell opposite the furnace?"

Eli nodded.

"That is 'Alpha Plan.' It connects to the street level." Wycliffe scratched his head. "Indeed, it may have worked if not for the Feds discovering our one deficiency."

A small explosion tore the trapdoor into shreds and sent shards of metal and wood to the cement floor below.

"Down!" shouted Eli as he hovered over Lizzy.

In the next minute, a thick, heavy rope fell through the trapdoor and Federation troops began descending, their dark uniforms blending into the room's background and their weapons catching an occasional shimmer of light from the glowing meters.

"We are completely unarmed!" cried Annie. "What shall we do?"

Instantly, Wycliffe drew a small handgun from his trouser pocket. "I am *never* unarmed!" He began shooting at the troops, picking several off as their boots touched the surface of the utility room.

Then, light flooded in from the main door through which they had just passed. Flashes of gunfire filled the entryway as James Winger and the men of the Harbor filtered through. But, gunfire forced them back through the doorway as more Feds slid down the rope as if it were a fire station pole.

Annie lifted her head slightly to see what was happening. She could make out the faces of James Winger and the kitchen helper Ralph. They were blasting their weapons as best they could but they were held off by the troops that kept coming down the rope. Soon, over twenty Federation soldiers infiltrated the room.

Then, throwing open the entryway door, Winger and his men forced their way into the utility room. Wycliffe was covering from behind as the Harbor men ducked behind barrels and shot from behind generators. Winger and Ralph managed to firefight their way to where Wycliffe and the others were ducked behind the barricade.

"Guess we didn't figure on them finding 'the hole'," yelled Winger to Wycliffe.

"What about the others? Did anyone get out by way of the tunnel?" asked Wycliffe.

"Yeah! The whole west end got out just in time!"

"Mr. Wycliffe, may I suggest I utilize your weapon—my eyesight is extremely acute in the darkness." Eli had crawled next to Wycliffe with his hand outstretched.

"An excellent idea, Eli." Wycliffe handed over his gun.

Immediately, Eli began picking off Federation soldiers but for every one he hit, two more dropped through the ceiling.

"I lost six of my men just getting here!" shouted Winger.

"We are definitely up against greater odds! It's only a matter of time before they overpower us!" answered Wycliffe.

"I know—we can't hold them off forever!"

The barrage of gunfire continued as more of Winger's men fought their way to the cement barriers.

"We're outnumbered!" shouted one of the Harbor men.

"There's nothing left for us! They'll overrun us in minutes!"

The gunfire continued, Eli picking off those who weren't crouching behind something. Then, the entire group of Federation soldiers seemed to organize on cue and converged on the cowering escapees. Eli hit several, but the majority of the troops were now within feet of the cement barricade. Lizzy began crying and Annie screamed as one of the Feds drew close enough to grab her by the strap of her handbag. "Help!" Annie screamed as the soldier's hand began to cover her mouth.

Then, sparks began to fill the room—incredible sparks like brilliant fireworks in the night sky. A high-pitched whirring sound vibrated the smoke-filled air. Annie looked up at the soldier who held her in a death grip. In the light of the dazzling sparks her eyes filled with terror and her mouth dropped open.

***

Jack Flint hit the ground running when he felt the soil of Central Park beneath his boots. He sprinted for the bombed-out brick shelter Garcia had pointed out moments before and where some of the others were waiting. Hefting his AKS easily off his shoulder, he held it in a ready-for-anything position. Crouching down in the shadow of the shelter, Jack waited for White and Com Two. In less than a minute, the entire team joined him as, together, they watched the heliplane lift from the ground, its massive rotors beating the summer air.

"Look smart and be alert," said Capt. Garcia in a low voice. "There's scrappers just waiting for us to leave our cover. In fact, they may not even—" A chilling scream erupted from a pile of debris twenty feet away and fifteen scrappers ran toward them like crazed lunatics. "This is it. Pick 'em off!"

Skeen began shooting and the high-pitched whine of his AKS filled the air. He picked five scrappers off before Jack got off a round. The horrific war hoops sent shivers down Jack's spine but he fought to stay focused. The last scrapper fell when more shrieks came from the left through a burned-out stand of trees. But, this group was different—it was returning fire.

"Get behind the building!" shouted Garcia, leading the way behind the brick structure. "These guys mean business but we have more firepower! Give 'em all you've got!" Garcia was shooting even bursts of ammo from his AKS. They were well-placed as five or six scrappers fell almost at once.

"They're crazy! They don't have a chance!" screamed Jack.

"They have the numbers!" shouted Garcia. "Keep 'em busy!"

Just then, Jack could see a band of scrappers coming through the trees from another direction. They seemed to have a leader who was shouting orders to the rest. Jack gripped his AKS tighter as they came into full view; each was armed with an automatic weapon, painted in old-time camouflage.

The leader was wearing a filthy gray shirt which did nothing to hide the bizarre tattoos which covered his face, arms, and chest. Thick leather bands wound around his wrists and neck. His black greasy hair jutted offensively from his scalp in pointed spikes. But, the thing that caught Jack's attention most was the ugly, red slash high on his neck. Dried blood and dirt were caked in a diagonal line from his Adam's apple almost to his ear. That bloody gash was familiar to Jack—one he had seen before, high above the Atlantic Ocean in the heliplane. "Don't shoot the leader!" screamed Jack almost hysterically. "He knows where Annie is! Com Two!"

"I hear you!" yelled Ethan Dibble. He was busy with his own firefight somewhere behind Jack. "Spare the leader!" screamed Dibble at the other members of the team.

"Yes, sir!" It was Capt. Garcia who answered and then gave the order to the others. Shots rang out and screams as the scrappers tried to surround the Coalition team.

"Bane! Look out!" shouted one of the rushing mob. But, the warning came too late. The scrapper named Bane had come too close to the corner of the brick shelter. Cpl. White stepped into the sunshine and with one mighty swing whacked Bane in the side of the head with his AKS. Bane dropped to the ground like a limp dishrag. Dragging Bane's unconscious form into the shadows, White shouldered the scrapper's weapon and returned to the task of picking off the enemy.

"Good work, White!" shouted Garcia.

Suddenly, everything went silent.

"Where'd they go?" shouted Parrish.

"We got their leader," answered Garcia. "They're probably regrouping." Garcia gave the order to retreat into the shadows on the far side of the structure. With White, Parrish and Skeen as lookouts, the group took a moment to regroup.

"Let's take a look at this bloke, Jack," said Com Two. Jack hovered over the still form of the scrapper called Bane who lay unconscious by a pile of bricks.

Jack examined Bane's neck. "It was in the time signature I saw on the heliplane, sir. It's unmistakably the same knife slash that I saw!"

"I believe you, Jack. But, let's keep a sharp eye on him. I don't know what value he can be to us—quite doubtful he would say anything to help us."

"Yes, sir, but he might be able to tell us if he's seen Annie and Eli."

Just then, Bane began to stir, lifting his hand to his head with a guttural moan.

"Don't move." The order came from Cpl. White. He was sitting on a large rock with his weapon propped on one raised knee and trained directly at Bane.

"In a few minutes, you'll be surrounded by ten more gangs. Hey, we have nothin' better to do," mumbled Bane, rubbing his head.

Jack moved closer. "In a few minutes you'll be dead if you don't—"

"I'll take it from here, Jack," said Com Two calmly. Dibble leaned against the rock where White sat, took off his cap momentarily and scratched his head. "Young man, I am in need of information." He sighed deeply, glaring intensely at Bane. "Have you seen a young woman with long, light-brown hair, blue eyes, slight of frame? She would have been traveling with a young man, a little over six feet tall, dark eyes, dark hair, slim build?"

"Sooo, the 'Govenah' seeks a young woman, 'slight of frame' does 'e," replied Bane, mocking Com Two's British accent.

In two long strides, Com Two was at Bane's side, a handgun at the scrapper's head and his boot to the man's throat. Dibble's voice was even and low. "Let me simplify things—who gave you that scar?"

"All right—lay off, man! Yeah, yeah, the girl and the dude you described. He practically slit my throat!" Bane scowled and spat out the information as if it were poison.

"*When* did you see them?" pressed Com Two.

"I dunno—last night? Maybe two nights ago—man, leave me alone! More of us are comin'—and soon."

"Where did they go?" Com Two pushed harder with his boot.

"There was a big fight. The blue men took 'em."

"Who are the blue men?" Com Two drew his face to within inches of Bane's.

"The blue men! You know—the ones who live in the river! They took the girl and the dude down into the East River!"

"Into the river?"

"Yeah, and the rest of 'em, too."

"There were others?"

"Yeah, a bunch of kids. Now, will you leave me alone?" Bane swore and struggled slightly against Com Two's grip.

Dibble bit his lip. This scrapper had actually seen Annie and Eli being taken down into the river. It didn't make sense. But, it tracked with the time signature Jack Flint had shared with him on the heliplane. Had Annie and Eli and possibly others been abducted by an even more sinister gang and dragged to their deaths in the East River? Dibble turned his head to glare at Bane when a bullet whistled past his ear. Dropping to the ground, he ordered everyone to gather in.

"Listen, this skirmish is getting us nowhere. Garcia, get us ready for the time jump—quickly!" Com Two's glare at Bane warned him not to move a muscle.

"Yes, sir." Garcia withdrew his chronometer from his breast pocket as the others followed suit. The chronometers used in Tel Aviv had previously reset themselves and the other members of the mission had received machines set at the exact same coordinates. Garcia glanced around the circle of the Coalition team. "Ready?"

All heads nodded.

"Three, two, one . . ."

Bane's mouth dropped open when he saw five men disappear into thin air.

When Jack pushed down the dial on his chronometer, the same one he had used in Israel, he felt himself enter the familiar time 'tornado.' He was determined to keep his feet squarely on the ground when it seemed the entire world had turned to mush beneath him. Not only was he caught in a spinning vortex of lightning and fireworks, but he had the distinct feeling he was moving through light years of space. All his faculties fought for control. His instinct was to close his eyes until it was all over when into his view came a vision he had seen before. Murky water surrounded him and he thought he was going to suffocate from the heaviness of the scene. In the distance was an orange orb. Several people were walking in slow motion toward the orb. He fought mentally and physically to make out the meaning of what he was witnessing. Then, through the dreariness, he saw her. It was Annie, ashen and limp in the arms of Eli. It was the scene from his time signature.

Then, as quickly as the scene had appeared, it changed to a brilliant white room full of video screens and computer equipment. The light was so blinding, Jack grit his teeth and braced himself against the stark contrast from the moment before. Where had Annie and Eli gone?

He searched in every direction the time tornado would permit and then he saw her again. Standing directly in front of him was Annie. Her form was taking a more solid shape until Jack could see that her arms were flailing against a soldier who had her locked in his firm grip. Why wasn't the tornado spitting him out? What was taking so long? He looked at the machine he still held in the palm of his hand. The dials were still spinning madly. He looked up and in that moment he caught Annie's eyes. There was clear recognition in her gaze as she looked up at him. Her mouth fell open in sheer amazement just as the spinning vortex abruptly ceased. The soldier gasped as he witnessed Jack materialize from nowhere. Jack felt a surge of energy as his right fist hit the soldier squarely in the jaw and sent him flying into the cement barricade of the Harbor utility room.

When the soldier's grip dropped from Annie, she staggered, stunned as Jack stood before her in the man's place. Losing her balance, she fell into Jack's arms. Swooping her up, he carried her behind the protective cement wall behind which Wycliffe and the others were crouching. The other members of the Coalition team were materializing all over the room where they immediately began picking off Federation soldiers. Two soldiers were descending down the thick rope from the trapdoor in the ceiling. Jack looked up to see several Feds glaring down from the gaping hole in the ceiling, getting ready to join those already on the rope. He saw Eli shooting and screamed. "Eli, cover me!"

Eli nodded, still picking off Federation soldiers around the utility room.

Jack took aim and shot at the two soldiers who were nearing the bottom of the rope. The Feds that were ready to descend felt gunfire from below and pulled their heads back. Jack saw his moment and, slinging his AKS around his shoulders with the strap, he ran across the room dodging gunfire until he reached the rope. As he jumped on, he began inching his way upward.

Garcia and the others kept picking off soldiers from the ground while Eli covered the Feds at the top of the rope. Jack pulled with all his might, inching closer and closer to the top. When he was within a few feet of the ceiling, he drew his Coalition-issued knife from its case and began sawing on the rope. Within seconds, the rope /w++as down to a few strands. With one final swipe, Jack severed it. Jack took in a deep gasp as he suddenly felt himself go weightless in his plummet to the floor. He landed with a thud, the rope falling in a heap on top of him.

At that instant, the Harbor men at the door took advantage of the lull in the action. They flooded into the utility room from the doorway and in seconds the last shots rang out. Garcia's men checked to see that there were no more Feds coming through the hole in the ceiling. The opening was dark and still. Soon everyone was gathered safely around the barricade.

"Jack!" Annie ran to him as he began to rise from the floor. "Are you all right?"

"Yeah, but I'm going to have a doozie of a headache," he replied, rubbing his forehead. Jack peeled himself away from the rope and gave it a toss into the corner. "Did that soldier hurt you?" Then, hardly thinking, he pulled Annie into his arms.

"I'm all right now," answered Annie. "More than all right." She looked up at Jack and searched his eyes. Then, Jack released her when he saw Com Two approaching from behind the barricade.

"Annie!" Ethan Dibble had worked his way to the end of the barricade where Jack had pulled his daughter to safety.

"Dad!" Annie ran to her father and buried her face in his shoulder.

"Annie, thank goodness you're safe."

James Winger sat with his head down, fighting to catch his breath. Eli was still gathered with Lizzy, Cory, and Preston, and Nicolas Wycliffe was returning his handgun to a holster hidden in his waistband.

"There's been an apparent lull in the fighting," stated Wycliffe. He stood up and his face caught the dim light of a meter dial.

Jack gasped. "H-how can this be?"

Wycliffe smiled. "I'm assuming that you're Jack Flint."

"And . . . and are you by any chance Nicolas Wycliffe? I mean, you sure look like him."

"Jack, how could you know what Nicolas Wycliffe looks like?" asked Annie.

"Because I flipped through one of his books a couple of days, I mean, hours . . . or . . . well, anyway—I saw one of his books with his picture on the back cover at Pole Star."

"Well, if I ever get my hands on that book, it should be an interesting read," said Wycliffe with a smile. "Especially since, in my view, it hasn't been written, yet. In the meantime, I suggest we get out of here." He addressed Com Two. "Commander, have you a plan for our retreat?"

"Indeed—Capt. Garcia, quickly inform everyone of our escape plans."

Garcia inched forward. "There are six chronometers and we'll take you up to the heliplane six at a time. Wycliffe, you and your group can go first with Annie, Eli, and the children. Your men can come on the second shift. Is that clear?" Garcia looked at Wycliffe's puzzled face.

"Well, first there are some things I must retrieve from my laboratory—don't worry—it won't take long. And, then . . ." Wycliffe hesitated and frowned.

"What is it?" asked Garcia.

"Well, I confess I am terrified of flying." He coughed. "Um . . what *exactly* is a heliplane?"

Eighteen

"What day is it?" asked Annie Dibble, shielding her eyes from the brilliant sunlight. The sky over Norway was azure blue and the opaque outline of the moon hung in the eastern sky.

"The 17th of August," replied Jack Flint. He led Annie up the steep trail where he had run up the Norwegian mountain just two days before. His foot set several rocks tumbling down the almost sheer rock face.

"This is scary," said Annie.

"But, look at that view—almost as beautiful as back home."

"You mean Rattlesnake Wash?"

"Yeah." Jack stood on the mountainside overlooking the fjord below. "But, it's different. There's no ocean in the distance in Idaho. And, those mountains as they meet the fjord—I've never seen anything to match it."

"I know." Annie turned to take in the view. Her skirt flapped gently against her legs from the breeze and she reached up to pull her hair back from her face. "It seems as though we've been gone away from home for ever so long."

"Anxious to get back?"

"I'm not sure. I . . . I've learned so much since I've been here—especially about my father." Annie closed her eyes and took in a deep breath. "I can't bear to leave him."

"You can look him up when you get back."

"But, dare I?" Annie turned to Jack. "I'm terrified that I might upset things . . . I mean, what if I slipped and said something that made my father choose differently." She was silent for a moment. "Oh, it's all so complicated."

"Yeah, it is." Jack motioned for Annie to follow and they began moving up the trail. In a few minutes, they came to the summit where Jack and the other Coalition members had rested from their run for a water break. He chose a large, flat boulder that overlooked the fjord and the valley below and sat down. "Hey, let me see that arm of yours."

Annie joined Jack on the rock and pulled the sleeve of her sweater above her elbow and extended her arm. "As you can see, there is absolutely no evidence of any injury."

"Eli told me you had serious blood poisoning."

"I did and I confess it was the worst pain I'd ever experienced."

"So, what did Timna do to heal it?" Jack withdrew a bag of peanuts from his shirt and offered them to Annie.

"Thanks... well, as I started to tell you yesterday, we were being accosted by those horrible dregs of humanity—"

"The scrappers?"

"Yes, horrible men, that is, if you can call them that."

"Yeah, we had our *own* run in with 'em."

"Well, before James Winger and his men arrived, Eli gave Timna to me. I don't even remember because I was quite unconscious at the time. He sort of folded her into the crook of my arm and she stayed there for a while. Even Eli doesn't know how exactly she works her little miracles. If she could speak, I'm confident she would tell me." Annie smiled.

"When I saw the condition of New York and those scrappers, I just had to have faith that you were in good hands with Eli. He's a pretty amazing guy."

"You never witnessed him fighting hand-to-hand with those gangs—his strength is quite remarkable." Annie looked thoughtfully down at her arm. "And, no one has told me not to reveal this to you— but, Jack, he can do fantastic things."

"Like swim underwater with no breathing device?"

"No, we all had breathing devices that got us through what Nicolas calls 'the tunnel'."

"Then, what?"

"I saw him put his hand on walls and disable entire electronic systems, or at least the alarm system. Then, when we were escaping through the main doors of the Federation building, he put his hand on a glass barrier. His hand began to glow and..."

"What?"

"Jack, that glass barrier stopped the soldiers' bullets as we ran for our escape. How do you explain that?"

"You don't." Jack looked at Annie. "You just call it 'classified'."

"Indeed. And, I wonder what else is 'classified' about our friend, Eli."

"We may never know." Jack rose from the rock and stretched.

"At any rate, I'm glad we found you—uh, everyone safe." Jack coughed and scratched his head. "I mean, the rescue mission . . . the Coalition team . . . I mean, it was a success."

Annie smiled and pulled her handbag from her shoulder. "Right you are. You certainly did show up in the nick of time." She opened her handbag and reached inside.

"Interesting choice of words."

"Would you like an apple? I stole one from the breakfast table this morning."

"Sure. You got enough?"

"I also have an orange and a banana." Annie threw Jack a shiny red apple which he easily caught. "And, Jack, I must ask you—whatever put it into your mind to climb that rope and sever it? You might have been killed!"

"And, during what part of that day could I *not* have been killed?" asked Jack.

"I suppose." Annie giggled.

"What's so funny?"

"I can't help but reflect on the astonished look on Garcia's face when you accomplished the task. He was speechless!"

"You know what he said?"

"What?"

"He said I almost reminded him of Com One when I jumped onto that rope."

Annie was listening intently.

"Then, he told me my boots were disgusting and I'd better get them spit shined before morning." Jack shook his head. "The guy just can't give it up."

Annie nodded her head and gazed out over the huge expanse of the fjord.

"And, wasn't it amazing how Winger's men fought their way from the river through the crowd of scrappers? They got to the heliplane just in time," said Jack.

"Oh, yes, I was so afraid for them. Nicolas said there was a group of them who escaped through the tunnel—I'm ever so glad they made it before we took off from the Park."

Just then, the sound of footsteps and pebbles tumbling down the mountain reached them.

"Helloooo!"

"Sounds like Wycliffe," said Jack. He walked part way down the trail and saw Nicolas Wycliffe picking his way gingerly up the mountain trail. He was wearing heavy hiking boots, a Coalition tee shirt and short cargo pants. When he saw Jack, he grinned and waved.

"Hello, Jack! Might I join you?"

"Of course. We're just munching on some treasure Annie found in her bag of bags which, I might add, has just about everything except the kitchen sink."

"Wonderful bag, that," said Wycliffe. "Why, when we evacuated the Harbor, she was generous enough to let me fill it with my lab stuff. Invaluable resource!"

Minutes later, all three were sitting on the flat boulder, eating crackers, cookies and fruit from Annie's bag.

"Anyone thirsty?" asked Jack.

"I finished my last bottle of water half an hour ago," admitted Annie.

"Wait here." Jack walked a few steps away and reached behind a large rock. Instantly, the rock opened and revealed the contents of the well-stocked refrigerator. "Drinks, anyone?"

"Delightful place, this Norway, isn't it? I mean, refrigerated rocks and all. I think I might stay awhile." Wycliffe bit into a muffin Annie had given him and took a swig of fruit juice from the cooler.

"Well, it's a far cry from New York City," replied Annie. She paused and looked at Wycliffe.

"Nicolas, just how did you come to be at the Harbor . . . and, how long were you there?"

"Well, I was actually there for less than two weeks."

"How on earth were you able to accomplish so much? I mean, the laboratory and all."

"Oh, the laboratory! That's easy to explain." Wycliffe took another drink and looked out over the valley. "It was already there. I simply reprogrammed the computer with data I had in my head. Winger and his men were extremely cooperative and willing to comb the city for the things I needed."

"What things did you need?" asked Jack.

"Why, materials for my inventions. I cannot simply sit still and not invent. I suppose you might say my brain is in a constant state of 'invention overload.' Ideas for new inventions simply flow into my brain—it's sort of an invention magnet. Hence, the desire for the Federation to kidnap and control me." Wycliffe laughed.

"What is it?" asked Annie. She drew her legs up and rested her chin on her knees.

"The irony of it all is that what the Federation is trying to do simply won't work. I mean, the inventive mind must have freedom from restraint. The minute force is employed, why, my mind turns into a lump of jelly! That's why living on the moor is so conducive to freedom of thought—the quiet and the boredom—one idea links arm in arm with another and then another until . . . well, the brainchild is born! Compulsion is, indeed, unfertile soil for sowing intelligence."

"Nicolas—may I call you that?" Jack felt a little foolish around someone who was at genius levels.

"Of course—I'm hardly Einstein, you know."

"Maybe not yet. But, what I wanted to know is something about my last time jump—when we materialized in the Harbor. Something was different. I was fighting to stay on my feet, but it really blew me over."

"I can explain. You see, as I was remotely—that is, from New York City— feeding data into the chronometers you used in Tel Aviv, I had infused them with GPS coordinates. I'm sure you remember the spinning dials."

"Yeah, that really freaked out Lt. Shaw."

"Well, the added information gave them the capability of transporting the bearer not only chronologically but physically—to a time destination and a physical destination. It took added minutes to lock on to the physical coordinates and, as a result, you probably felt as though you'd been spit out of a cyclone."

"Worse."

"Well, anyway, I hope that answers your question."

"Nicolas, where do we go from here?" asked Annie. She began putting empty water bottles in her handbag. "What about the experiences of the past few days? They're sure to affect our lives when we go back to our original time."

"Yes, I've had some experience with that. The things we've seen and heard, the friendships we've made—they must have the least degree of impact when we go back to the past. It takes a tremendous amount of self-control not to reveal the future to our family, to our friends. Do you think you can do that?"

"I . . . I don't know—I certainly hope so, that is, if you think it's important."

"Annie, Jack—you must believe me when I say it's important. You've seen the future—you've caught a glimpse of your future selves, literally. The trick will be to let it work for you and not against you. Let it lift you to greater heights. You would never have been timesnatched in the first place if you weren't going to make a mark on this world—a mark for good." Wycliffe smiled. "Actually, we've all been given a great gift—the chance to see our true potential. Maybe in some cases, a chance to choose differently."

Jack tucked in his shirt. "So, when do we make the jump?"

"My father told me we must prepare for the return trip tomorrow morning," replied Annie softly.

***

Nicolas Wycliffe, Annie Dibble, and Jack Flint sat around a table in the Pole Star cafeteria and ate in silence. It was nine-thirty a.m. the next morning and they were due to meet Com Two in his office at ten for the time jump. Nicolas had infused the chronometers not only with their time destinations but with each of their physical destinations. Jack lifted his eyes and met Annie's gaze.

"So, do you have everything? Especially that bag of yours?"

"Yes." Annie was dressed in the same clothing she came in the day Finke took her.

"It's most important that you take nothing with you from this time level," stated Wycliffe.

"Yeah, we understand. I had nothing—"

"Except these." Wycliffe reached into his pocket and set three bohrium bracelets on the table between the water glasses.

"Why are they different?" asked Annie. "I've always ever seen them to be purely smooth as glass."

"I confess I was quite busy last night. Your father allowed me to visit the base laboratory and, well, I had some ideas on improving the bracelets that I couldn't wait to try. There was a supply of bohrium in the laboratory and I learned a great deal with some experiments."

Jack picked one up and turned it over in his hands, examining it in detail. Instead of being one band of smooth silver metal, Wycliffe had created a bracelet comprised of what looked to Jack like a mesh of silver ball bearings. There were several rows of tiny balls, each alternating with the row next to it, creating a woven effect. It was light and slipped easily over his hand. "What makes it better?"

"For one thing, there's no need to remove them with the blue light. The unique properties of bohrium allow them to fit the wearer perfectly and they adapt to the size of the wrist. I also discovered an interesting property of the element when it is in the tiny spherical form you see here." Wycliffe removed his own bracelet and pointed out the tiny silver balls that made up the band. "I discovered while wearing mine that when I reached for a chronometer, the bracelet began to vibrate. I don't know to what use that will be, but it's an interesting fact to be aware of."

"They're quite lovely," remarked Annie. She picked hers up and smiled, turning it over before she slipped it on.

"And, just how am I going to explain to the Sheriff why I'm wearing a bracelet?" Jack frowned and shook his head.

"You just escaped from Federation Headquarters, time jumped to save your future self, and won a horrific battle with those horrible scrappers in New York City—I'm sure you'll think of something," said Annie as she rolled her eyes.

Jack looked at her and raised his eyebrow.

"Let me show you something," said Wycliffe. He reached over to Jack's bracelet and pulled it higher on his arm. The bracelet automatically adjusted to the size of Jack's upper arm. "If you don't want people to see it, you can also wear it around your ankle." Wycliffe pulled up his sleeve to reveal his own bracelet. "Since Finke is a threat, we must always wear these."

Just then, Cpl. White entered the room. "I'm here to escort you to Com Two's office, sir."

"Thanks, White."

Jack, Annie, and Nicolas followed Cpl. White through the ground floor of Pole Star. Their route took them through the spacious lobby Jack and Annie had first encountered and where they had first met Lt. Shaw. They continued on to the elevators and to the hallway beyond where they soon stood before Com Two's office.

When they entered the room, Jack was surprised to see so many people gathered. Capt. Garcia stood with strict military bearing to Ethan Dibble's left. Lizzy, Cory and Preston were sitting in the corner of the room by the television screen, quietly talking. Skeen and Parrish stood by the windows and James Winger looked up when they entered the room.

"Nick—it's good to see you again. I mean, before you have to go back," said Winger.

"I know that we met on this time level, James, but it is most probable that we will cross paths again in the future. I certainly hope so." Wycliffe shook Winger's hand. "I could not have accomplished what I did without your help. Many thanks to you and your crew. You will tell them for me, won't you?"

"You bet."

At that moment the door swung open and Eli entered the room. He was back in his crisp Coalition uniform and his dark hair was trimmed impeccably. He reached into his pocket.

"I thought you might want to say goodbye to Timna." He held the little creature out to Annie.

"Thank you, Eli." Annie stroked Timna's tiny head with her forefinger and pulled her close to her cheek. "Dear little thing." Timna gave a little shake and snuggled down into the palm of Annie's hand.

"Eli, I wish I could have seen you in action, but maybe another day," said Jack.

"Flint, you *have* seen me in action. You have no idea what lies in store in your future. Until then, I wish you all the best." Eli saluted.

"I guess you're right." Jack awkwardly returned the salute. "I'll do my best to live up to your expectations."

"My expectations have already been realized. God speed, my friend."

"Thanks."

Com Two left his desk and joined the group. He put his arm around Annie's shoulder. "I believe it's time," he said quietly.

Annie reached up to kiss her father's cheek. "Dad, what shall I say to you when I get back? I mean, may I come live with you?"

Ethan Dibble looked into his daughter's eyes. "Annie." He struggled for words. "Annie, when you get back, give me some time. Give me some time to . . . to figure things out."

Annie touched her father's face, tears swimming in her eyes. "All right." She took a deep breath. "I shall remember this moment—I shall remember when I looked into the face of Commander Two." She forced a smile. "That will give me courage to be patient."

"Thank you, my dear." Dibble hugged his daughter tightly. "All right, then," he said as he cleared his throat. "Let me have your strict attention. First off, everyone has been issued a bohrium bracelet—they should be stowed in a pocket or satchel in order for the time jump to be possible. When you reach your time destination, I implore you to wear the bracelet at all times for security measures.

"Now then, each of you will be escorted to your proper time level and place, dropped off—so to speak—and, then, the escort will return here. Is that understood?"

Everyone nodded.

"Good. Let's see, then, Annie—I'll be your escort. Jack, Capt. Garcia will be yours."

At the mention of Garcia as his escort, Jack flinched but said nothing. He glanced toward the captain who stood at Com Two's desk with no reaction.

"Nicolas, James will be your escort," Dibble continued, "Lizzy, Eli will accompany you. Cory, Sgt. Skeen will escort you, and Preston, Cpl. White will be your escort. Is everyone clear?"

Again, everyone nodded. Lizzy smiled up at Eli who gazed down into her brown eyes. Garcia began making his way toward Jack, and the others began to group accordingly. Then, Jack went to Annie's side where she was standing by her father.

"Well, I guess this is goodbye," said Jack. He looked down at Annie and arched one eyebrow.

"I truly hope we shall meet again—perhaps through the Coalition or . . ." Annie's sentence trailed off into nothing.

Jack thought about the collage of pictures back in Com One's office. "Let's let time take care of it."

Annie stared into Jack's steel-gray eyes, not knowing what to say.

"I'll try to be there the *next* time you get in trouble, which is actually quite often." Jack smiled and gave her a gentle hug.

"I'll be counting on it." Annie replied softly.

Then, Jack walked a few feet away back to where Capt. Garcia was standing.

"Capt. Garcia, will you kindly give us the order?" stated Com Two.

"Yes, sir." Garcia turned toward the group. "Is everyone's chronometer ready?"

All heads nodded.

"All right, let's go." Garcia raised his chronometer. "Ready, three, two—"

The door to Com Two's office flew open.

"Com Two, wait!" shouted Lt. Shaw. Wisps of hair were sticking out of her usually perfect bun and her face was flushed.

"Lt. Shaw, what is it? We were nearly gone in the time jump!" responded Com Two.

"Something has come in from our Intel division at FOPS. Here's the report."

Com Two slipped his chronometer into his uniform pocket and walked toward Lt. Shaw, reaching for the report she held. He scanned the paper and motioned for Wycliffe to join him. "Take a look at this, Nicolas."

Nicolas Wycliffe reached for the paper in Com Two's hand. During the thirty seconds it took him to read it, his mouth dropped open. "Oh, dear."

Capt. Garcia turned to Com Two. "What is it, sir?"

"That renegade, that dimwit called Robert Finke is on a time rampage, creating all kinds of havoc. What is your opinion, Wycliffe?"

Wycliffe slipped off his glasses and chewed on the stem, his eyebrows furrowed. "Simply put, Commander, this changes everything."

"In what manner?"

"In an extremely complicated manner, sir—one which would take me hours to explain in detail."

"Then, render the simplest explanation possible."

"May I borrow something first?" Wycliffe didn't wait for an answer but his long legs took him to Com Two's coffee table where a thick book with a shiny red and black cover sat near a potted plant. He picked up the book and began leafing through its many pages.

In the minutes it took him to find what he was looking for, everyone in the room began whispering and glancing at each other. Finally, Wycliffe looked up from the pages. "Here it is—Forgive me for quoting from my own future publication, but I was just studying this last night and now it will prove very useful indeed to us."

"Go ahead," said Com Two.

"May I quote from page 242 . . . *"Regarding the subject of time trails, it has been my experience that every individual who has moved about on the time continuum establishes a time trail. In some individuals, this trail is extremely prevalent. In others, it barely manifests itself. Nevertheless, I repeat that a time trail is embedded into every individual who enters the realm of time movement. As a result, each trip backward and forward into time leaves a trail, a wake that influences the wakes of others. To complicate matters, entering time levels crosses wake over wake, creating confusion in the time sequence of the quantum leap necessary for the—"*

"That's probably enough, Wycliffe," said Com Two quietly. He clasped his hands behind his back and paced before his desk. The room was silent but for the ticking of the pendulum clock in the corner. Eli sat with Lizzy on the sofa softly stroking Timna's tiny head. Jack glanced at Annie and shrugged his shoulders, and Capt. Garcia stood stiffly, almost at attention, next to the flagpole by the window. Then, Com Two halted his pacing and turned again to the boy scientist. "I need your best assessment."

Nicolas Wycliffe returned his spectacles to his face, scratched his nose and ran his fingers through his unruly cowlick. "The report reads that Robert Finke was flung haphazardly into the time continuum. His whereabouts are completely unknown, but his presence has been detected at a variety of time levels. Commander, this is nothing short of catastrophic in nature. Finke's movements intricately intertwine him with the time trails of every person in this room!" Wycliffe paused before he spoke again. "You have asked me for my assessment. That, sir, will not be an easy task, but I *will* say this . . ." His eyes drifted to Jack and Annie. "None of the 'time children' will be going back today. No, not today—and not at any time in the near future."

To Be Continued . . .

Coming Soon . . .

Timesnatched:
Southern Cross

About the Author

Barbara Boyle spent twenty years traveling the world with her husband and eight children in the U.S. Air Force. She now lives with her husband in Idaho where she spends her sunny days writing novels for her grandchildren.

Learn more at:
www.bdboyle.webs.com

Also by the Author

The Return of Thomas Gunn
The Dillree Family History

Made in the USA
Monee, IL
29 July 2022